THE SERPENT'S EYE

Thomas H. Brand

<u>Also available from the author</u>

<u>Fiction</u>
The Æther Collection

<u>Non-Fiction</u>
A Basic Guide to Ethical Non-Monogamy

To Francesca,

I write these words in warning. Do not make my mistake. I fear should anyone start along my path that they will find their fate inexorable. As I have.

I am gone. He is me. I cannot burn this journal. I cannot. I should do so but his presence withholds my arm. Edgar at least made the attempt, but I am certain whatever agency saved his words will shield mine also. I will never be allowed such freedom. So close. He sees what I see. What I write. He knows, for he is me.

I am lost. I must hide this journal as best I can. My last act upon this earth is to write this warning: If you are reading these words, it means the sanctum I hoped would be eternal has been uncovered. I implore you, as your mind remains free, take the action that I cannot. See these pages burned. Disperse the ashes in some holy place. Flee. Pray.

If you cannot do this thing, if you find some power stays your hand, then please, I beg you, see that it is once again hidden. Let the unwitting souls of others be shielded, and then see about your own affairs. If this be the case, then I fear we have already met in that great stone corridor. Dark. Eternal. Forever.

I go to my end.

In the name of God

George Sandings
    January 4th 1817

Monday, April 8th 1816

Herein this journal are recorded the words of myself, George Bartholomew Sandings, attorney; working on the behalf of Caine and Dennings, Solicitors, at the behest of my client; Sebastian, Earl Leer.

This morning my ship has at last arrived at port in the good city of Buenos Aires, Argentina. The ocean voyage has been long, and as arduous as such an undertaking can be for one who has never before travelled beyond England's shores. But my companions upon this journey have been pleasant company, and through that companionship I found myself not too hard pressed by the enforced inaction of the voyage. However, I find no small gratitude in being once again ashore.

I have travelled here to this foreign land at the instruction of my employers, Messrs Caine and Dennings, to see to the probate of the late Earl Edgar Thomas Andrew Leer, who passed away within this city some time last year, and the settling of his business. Despite my position within the company as a mere junior associate, it has fallen upon me to act as legate and representative for the Leer family on this matter. It is a role I have accepted gratefully, showing as it does the favour my employers hold me in.

I was met at the wharf by my contact and guide; one Mr. Arthur Cartwright. He is a hearty, affable fellow, hailing from the hills of Wales of all places, though now settled and employed here within Buenos Aires. Whilst we waited for my baggage to be unloaded, and then again while making the journey to my lodgings, he regaled me with the tales of how he came to settle in a city so far away from his one time home. Upon leaving the army, which he tells me he joined in his youth as an escape from the farm life he was born to, he decided upon the southern Americas as a place to increase and enjoy his fortunes. After some travel about the continent he found himself here in Buenos Aires, though bereft of what moneys he had begun with. As he so readily enjoys telling me, rather than gain wealth as he intended, he instead lived life. And life was expensive. To his good fortune he took a liking to the city, as well as finding himself a wife who much settled him. He now makes a comfortable living by various means, not the least as a guide and contact for foreign visitors such as myself.

I find I like the fellow. Some years my senior, he is of an open disposition and has treated me like an old acquaintance from the off. Already I have found his assistance invaluable, as I have discovered my Spanish has deteriorated much since my school days. The people here speak at such a speed my ear cannot make sense of much more than the odd word, but with Cartwright's assistance I am confident I will soon regain much of my former knowledge. I have simply to be thankful that my parents insisted I learn the language in my youth so that I have this basis of knowledge on which to rebuild.

I have established myself in my modest lodgings; a fine, if plain, room in the house of one Señor Mercallo. My host is an amiable man, living here with his wife and son. He speaks a little English, and so with my halting Spanish we manage to communicate. I imagine they often rent out this room to travellers, as they seem understanding of the weaknesses I appear to be suffering after so long at sea.

I have unpacked my belongings and plan to take an early night. The sooner my recovery from this journey, the sooner I can be about my business.

Wednesday, April 10th 1816

It is now two days since I arrived in this city, and I finally begin to feel myself once more. Whilst I believed my constitution unaffected by my travels, upon disembarking I discovered I had become more acclimatised to sea travel than I had realised. It has taken these two days before I have been able to stand firm without the sensation of the ground lurching beneath me. A common complaint, I am told, for one having undergone their first major ocean voyage.

The city, as much as I have seen of it so far, is both strange and familiar. It is alike to London in many ways, or indeed any English city, and yet different in so many others. The people and their mannerisms are noticeably altered from my own race. They are not unpleasant, either to converse with or look upon, but being amongst them leaves me with an unavoidable sense of being a foreigner in this land.

There is little sign remaining here of the battles for independence still being fought in the north. I pray it remains that way for the duration of my stay. This country's struggles against its Spanish masters do give me some trepidation when walking the streets. I cannot say visiting a land in such a state of upheaval appeals to me, but the chance to further my prospects is great enough that I can brave such dangers as may be. My European stock has indeed aroused some interest in the streets, but my landlord seems a decent fellow and appears little concerned with my heritage. My rooms, at least, will provide me with a refuge from whatever hostility I may encounter.

I sit now in a most comfortable coffee house, recommended to me by Señor Mercallo. It is close by my lodgings and as fine a place as any to settle my legs and absorb the town's atmosphere. I have not had much of a taste for coffee before, but here it is stronger and more flavourful than that which I have tasted at home. Whilst I would prefer tea, I do feel I could develop a taste for this drink.

The swapping of the seasons is the strangest thing. It is April still, yet here I find myself in the last throws of summer. You can read about such global effects in any number of books, but to actually experience it is another thing. I am only glad I shall not be here more than a month, or else I might well have gone from one winter to another without the relief of summer!

I wish to be about my purpose as quickly as I may, and so, despite the lingering discomfort from the voyage, this morning I made my first approaches into the city. I have made appointments with city officials regarding my business for tomorrow at noon. As I fill in what time remains today enjoying the warmth of the afternoon weather, I shall recount, for the sake of this journal's completeness, the situation I have been sent to finalise.

Last autumn, the previous Earl Leer, Edgar Thomas Andrew, died whilst residing in this city. The late Earl was infamous for his life of exploration and adventure, amongst other aspects of his personality. It was not unexpected, nor unprepared for, that Earl Edgar's departure from this world to the next would not take place in England, for he spent very little of his life there. He was orphaned at a young age, as his father and mother both perished in the sinking of the *Endeavour* in 1759 when Edgar was not yet six years old. The young Earl then spent a childhood watched over by a series of guardians who presided over the family estates until Edgar's majority was reached.

I am given to understand that, as he grew, Edgar quickly gained a reputation for recklessness and a less than savoury manner. On his twenty-first birthday he took full control of the wealth of his estates and at once set off across the world with his young and, to the great dismay of the family, common-born wife, Margaret Elizabeth. The marriage was a great scandal at the time, but the exact details have been obscured by the family so I have been unable to discover a definitive story. Different rumours have her as either a maid at Oxford University, where he had been studying, or the niece of one of Edgar's tutors. I cannot comment on the validity of either rumour, merely recount them.

What is known is that the Earl's life was not that of a respectable man. While I demur from speaking ill of the dead whenever possible, I believe such an assertion cannot be avoided when recounting tales of Earl Edgar's life. Neither, by all accounts, did he make any attempt to hide or feel embarrassment from his reputation. He was a young man with no father to guide him, but with the riches of the Leer family at his disposal. One might say his swift fall into corruption can be understood, if not condoned. An excess of wealth and lack of a father's moral guidance would be too much for many good men, and the fact that even his notorious excesses across the whole breadth of the world did not fully bankrupt his family shows exactly what fortune he had at his disposal. In forty years he managed to spend most of it, but still enough remains for the family to be considered wealthy by common standards.

I can tell of only two occasions where Earl Edgar visited England. Twenty-seven years ago he returned to deliver his newborn son, Sebastian Edward, into the hands of those same guardians he had so despised, before leaving again almost on the same tide. There has been some speculation as to whether Edgar had fathered any children prior to this date, but no substantial claims of patrimony have ever been made. Sebastian was the first and only child the Earl acknowledged as his own. After that, I believe the Earl returned but once to his native land, ten years ago. For what purpose this was I am unsure.

Six years ago, soon after the death of his wife, Earl Edgar settled here in Buenos Aires. The cause of death for the Lady Margaret is as yet unknown, and it is one of my tasks to ascertain this so it can be marked in the family histories. What is known is that the Earl married again soon after, at the age of fifty-seven. He then ceased his travels and lived out his remaining years in the city. Also, if rumour is to be believed, he sired another son with this new wife.

Upon news of the Earl's death reaching England over the winter, Sebastian has wasted no time in taking control of his family's failing estates. The new Earl makes no secret of his hatred for his parents, their abandonment of him and their squandering of the Leer family fortunes. Since reaching his majority, he has champed at the bit to take control of his inheritance. I myself have been involved in a number of cases brought to the courts, all of which have been in vain. He has been forced to watch from afar as his father frittered his money away through a life of lavish excess. The Leer estates in Derbyshire were sold off when the new Earl was a child, and those that remain lie in disrepair.

Now we reach the purpose of my sojourn here in South America. Earl Sebastian wishes the probate of his father concluded at as swift a pace as possible. Also, as my employer Mr. Caine reminded me before I embarked, there is much in the way of the late Earl's past that must be clarified for the family histories. A family such as the Leers has been documented through the centuries, and Earl Edgar's life and travels have left a blank to blight that history. During my time here I am expected to learn whatever I can to rectify this.

I have a month in which to conclude my business, with passage home booked for the end of May. If all goes well, and I can conclude things swiftly, I hope I may have the chance to see more of this city and the surrounding country. This is my first trip overseas, and I wish to make the most of it. Other than joining the army, I cannot see any way I would otherwise have this opportunity.

I also have it in my head that making connections and friendships within the city might put me in a unique position within the firm, promoting my interests should Mr. Caine and Mr. Dennings have any future business here. This trip has provided me with a great opportunity to further my prospects, and I intend to see that I grasp it fully.

Thursday, April 11th 1816

This afternoon I had my first meeting with the local authorities of the town; a formal interview with the city magistrates to go over the records from last year regarding the late Earl's legal statuses.

There is a record of the Earl's second marriage; to one Maria Juanita Gonzalez, a maid some thirty-five years his junior, that took place a little over two months after the Earl's arrival in the city. There have been no records found of the Lady Margaret's death, so I must surmise this unfortunate event happened before the Earl's arrival within the city. Hopefully, once I have met with those who travelled in the Earl's circle, I will be able to discover more about the lady's fate. There is also a birth notice naming Earl Edgar and his young wife as parents of Tobias, a boy born little more than two years prior to the Earl's death.

I do not relish undertaking my interview with the widow. Rumours of her and her son's existence have long reached England's shores and found their way to the ears of Earl Sebastian. He has made it clear he neither recognises the marriage, nor the legitimacy of the child. He has already engaged my firm to deal with that matter, and in the English courts I imagine that by now all the legalities must be settled.

I pray this young lady has family she might rely on for the care of her child, as she shall find neither sympathy nor support from her husband's kin.

By the records of the city, of which I am now in possession of written copies, it seems the Earl's death was discovered on 29th July, 1815. I shall have to give myself time to read the witness statements in full, but the indication given is that the Earl's final days were not taken in a noble manner.

It is to my good fortune that the combination of the Earl's rank and his infamy around the city meant his death was notable, and so thoroughly examined at the time. I have much information on which to begin my report, and have acquired the names of those known to be close to the Earl whom I might interview myself. While I deal with these initial matters, and familiarise myself with the city, I can allow myself several days before seeking out the Earl's family.

Friday, April 12th 1816

As my time spent in this city goes on, I find myself liking it more and more. The home of Señor Mercallo is warm and his family most welcoming. The coffee shop to which he directed me on my first day has become much like a study. I find the city's humid warmth most agreeable, and am very happy to bask in it while I read those reports I have so far acquired.

Standing out as I do in this land of dark skin and hair, so unlike my own fair complexion, has brought me to the notice of the proprietor, one Pascal de Certona who, I have learnt from my landlord, owns the shop with his sister; a lady I have yet to meet as she is visiting family farther south. He speaks no English, and seems much amused by my halting Spanish. He welcomes me warmly upon each visit, and has bestowed upon me some name or title I cannot quite comprehend. Attempts to persuade him to use my given name have proven futile.

I also find a firm friendship growing with Arthur Cartwright; my rock of Britishness in this sea of exotic unfamiliarity. It amuses me that while he speaks Spanish like a native, upon reverting to his mother tongue his lyrical Welsh lilt returns as strong as ever. Last night he and his wife took me to a tavern he knows well where we were treated like family. Mrs. Cartwright is a native of this city, and one of the smallest women I have ever met. She appears quite incongruous sitting next to her rotund husband, but from the amount of wine she drank throughout the night, which little affected her manner, I have no doubt of her constitution. I myself must admit to feeling more than a little worse for wear this morning, but Señor Certona's wonderful coffee seems a tonic to my condition.

In my delicate state, I decided against further exploration of the neighbourhood and gave today over to reading through the reports I garnered yesterday in greater detail. It seems the late Earl, for all his uproarious youth and famed wanderlust, became somewhat of a recluse in his final years. He had apartments in the rich side of the town, and was noted for riotous parties and occasions held open to both notable and infamous alike. Unfortunately, as is often the case, the authors of these reports make vague mentions of people and events they assume the reader to have a previous familiarity with, and so certain details are omitted. I have made a note of what seems to be missing, and shall focus my research on these areas.

Last night, while we dined, Cartwright had begun to tell me some of what he knew of the matter, but Señora Cartwright made it clear she did not consider talk of the Earl such a thing to be discussed at the dinner table, so I learned frustratingly little other than that in the days running up to the discovery of the Earl's death he had been seen by no one. Indeed, he had become such a recluse that when news of the discovery of his body spread many were shocked, as they believed he had either fled the city or died already. I was very frustrated by Mrs. Cartwright's refusal to allow her husband to tell me more. I shall enquire further when next I see him.

For the relief of my curiosity these reports do tell me more on this front, albeit in a more clinical and succinct wording than Cartwright's telling. They record that Earl Edgar died alone in his apartments after a period of self-enforced isolation. The last time he had been seen by any witness had been a fortnight earlier, after which he locked himself in his chambers, refusing to speak with anyone. When bailiffs, called by those seeking redress for various debts, forced entry into the rooms they discovered the Earl's body. By the doctor's estimations he had been dead some days. His rooms were in disarray. In finding no sign of ingress save their own, the authorities concluded the damage was the Earl's own doing. Most likely caused in some fit of madness.

The official cause of death was recorded as a brain fever; likely brought about through some long contracted illness. Indeed, I know of several conditions prevalent amongst those men and women of moral disrepute and unsavoury character that are said to affect the mind after a number of years. Knowing of Earl Edgar's reputation, I cannot think it an unlikely or arguable cause of his demise.

I have now to write up my summary of the reports, and file copies for my return. It seems that perhaps my business may be concluded sooner than anticipated, should my intended interviews go well. Once I have spoken to those who were known associates of the Earl, and also sought out his widow's family, I shall have the chance to explore the city for my own education.

But this personal goal must be put off until my business is

done. Therefore, I shall be about my work.

Monday, 15th April 1816

This morning, having spent the weekend compiling my reports, I resolved to seek out the widow Maria Juanita Gonzalez. It is not a task I relish, for I fear that as a representative of her late husband's family it shall fall to me to crush any hopes she may have regarding her future. However, that is my charge and a Sandings shall not balk at a task once undertaken. I can only hope her current situation is not so desperate that my refusal of aid causes too great a distress to her and her child.

I took with me Arthur Cartwright, for, as a companion who knows both the language and customs of the town far better than I, I foresaw he would be most useful in this delicate situation. I feared that alone I might make some inadvertent *faux pas*, and his cultural knowledge could prove invaluable.

Together, we braved the walk to the address I had been given. The directions took us to the poorer district of the city, a good distance from my lodgings, and it took us most of the morning to reach it. Here the houses became smaller and more cramped, though not yet what I would deem the slums of the city. There are areas such as these back home in London, although even there I would be wary of entering while too finely dressed. They are the homes of the working folk, taking pride in their mean fortunes. But even in areas such as this may be found men and women happy to take advantage of those wealthy enough to take too little care of their wallet. While not offering much to any footpad, I felt still that I stood out as one unfamiliar to the area.

Men and women roamed the streets. Many glared as we passed and I will admit to suffering some nerves at this attention, but Arthur seemed unconcerned. He told me that while the British occupation of ten years ago is ill recalled by the people of the city, we should attract little outright aggression by our presence. Many in fact, he told me, have turned the anger felt at the attempted occupation away from the British and onto the Spanish masters the British looked to hurt, in order to build support for the struggle for independence. He has promised me that I am in no more danger than he himself.

Sometime before noon we came to the address we sought. The house was a nondescript, if well kept, building nestled in the middle of a cramped street. Nearby stood a church. Aside from a large and ornate crucifix adorning the entranceway to the otherwise plain building, there were no other notable landmarks to make this neighbourhood in anyway unique or distinctive.

We knocked upon the door of the house and found ourselves facing a small, dark, elderly woman in an outfit of sombre black. She peered up at the two of us as I haltingly introduced myself and my companion. She appeared suspicious of my accent but seemed to understand me well enough. However, upon my utterance of the name of my employer she unleashed a torrent of angry Spanish towards me, spoken at such a volume and speed that I was quickly lost, unable to pick up more than the occasional word. At various points in her tirade she would cross herself, in the way of Catholics, but never did that action hinder the speed or ferocity of her outburst.

Without Cartwright I would have truly floundered here. He seemed completely unfazed by such an outburst. I thought it some kind of hysteria, but he later explained that such a thing is common with women of this land. He told me that should I take an Argentinian wife, as he had, I would soon consider such things commonplace.

Eventually the old woman ran out of words and stood glaring up at me, standing defiant in the middle of the doorway. Cartwright then proceeded to summarise that which had been said. This indeed was the house of the widow's family, and the formidable lady before us was her mother, Señora Gonzalez. I shall not attempt to transcribe the exact words, though Cartwright took great pleasure in repeating the more colourful phrases verbatim. Suffice it to say, the mother's opinion of her daughter's late husband was not a high one. She blamed Earl Edgar for corrupting her daughter Maria, and leading her into a life of sin and evil. His death and her subsequent abandonment by his family was, in her mother's opinion, her only chance for salvation. She then swore in the names of a number of saints that she would not allow us to draw her daughter back into a life of fresh sin.

Upon hearing the translation, I restated the fact that I was simply an agent employed by the Leers, not a Leer myself, and that I sought nothing from the lady's family. I assured her I simply wished to speak to her daughter on the legal matters of her husband's death. Sensing it would be the best tack to choose, I stressed that once I had undertaken this task the Leer family would be done with Maria and likewise desired that there never be any future contact with her, her son or her family.

My assurances did little to appease this guardian of the threshold. Whether I was a devil, she informed me, or merely the emissary of devils, I was to stay away from her daughter lest I tempt her with sin and immorality as her husband had. Maria had made her confessions, she declared loudly, and was seeking forgiveness for her past sins.

Arthur was little help through this whole encounter. In fact he took a great deal of amusement from the diminutive harridan before us, and was grinning widely when she finally slammed the door in my face. As for myself, I was stunned at the vehemence of the reaction. To what depths had the Earl cavorted to cause such a hatred in the mother of his bride? Or was this simply the overprotectiveness of the Latin matriarch? I expressed my amazement, but Cartwright merely laughed, claiming I did not understand the ways of Buenos Aires women if I thought this anything out of the ordinary.

At this point I found myself feeling most conspicuous; standing out as we did in this suburb of the city. I looked around, and could clearly see a number of eyes regarding us from doorways and windows. Señora Gonzalez's words had not been circumspect, and it was only to be expected that they would have drawn attention. While Arthur had been an inhabitant of this land for years enough that I had no doubt, should he wish to, he could easily blend in with these surroundings, I was under no illusions I appeared anything other than the trespassing European.

Given her words regarding confession and repentance it occurred to me that my target might well have been in the nearby church, but by then my urge to leave this place was greater than my desire to be thorough. I felt at any moment the locals might well accost us, taking me for an invader of their home soil. I now wince at the cowardice I felt at the time, but could distinctly feel their eyes on the back of my neck and had no compunctions about leaving the district and returning to the city proper.

Chastising Cartwright for his growing mirth at my situation, I led him back the way we had come and resolved to return on some later occasion. I am not yet pressed for time, and shall resume my attempt at interviewing the widow on another day. One where I might better prepare myself for what I face.

As if sensing my despondence at having been so summarily cast from my quest, and once his amusement had calmed, Cartwright has promised to investigate further on my behalf. Being able to blend in with the locals more readily than I, he has promised to enquire as to the widow Maria's habits and customs that I might intercept her at some innocuous place well away from the vile custodian whom had blocked my way.

Thursday, 18th April 1816

Having failed in my design on Monday, and having dispatched Arthur Cartwright to begin his own investigations on my behalf, on Tuesday morning I resolved to continue my work within the closer areas of the city. I hoped I might have greater luck in the more metropolitan surroundings than had I found in the outskirts.

By all accounts, Earl Edgar had been a well known personage in the city from the first. The arrival and settlement of a British Earl in the city so soon after the occupation had been cause enough for some note, and his actions and lifestyle in the following years did little to assuage his infamy.

These past few days I have spent following up my list of possible contacts in the hope they might be more prepared to speak with me. I must now record that most doors in the city have been shut in my face. It seems most do not wish to discuss their one time associations with the Leer name. Thankfully a few sources have been more forthcoming, and through this testimony I have been able to glean what is at least a fragmentary history of the Earl's life here. I will attempt to recount it in a more linear form, at least for the purpose of understanding it better myself.

Earl Edgar arrived here in Buenos Aires sometime in the October of 1810. This, at least, I had already known. He immediately procured apartments for himself and his retainers, hired what staff he required, and began making himself known.

It would seem he quite rapidly became a figure of some repute. At first, with the political climate as it was at that time, his nationality engendered no small amount of suspicion. This, it seems, the Earl overcame through the liberal application of wealth. He made no attempts at frugality, spending lavishly both at his home and around the town. Soon the promises of fortune and good times eroded any harsh feelings that there may have been towards him from any but the most puritan of the city's fellows. It was clear he had little care for international politics, or in any possible interests the British Empire might have had in the city, and his name soon became a feature of city gossip.

Ever an unpredictable fellow, the Earl was known as one who might appear at any establishment about town, be it high class or low. While one night he might have held a grand banquet in his apartments and invited all the great and good to attend, the next he could as easily have been found carousing and brawling in the taverns with the lowest ranks of society.

I sought first to introduce myself to those families of a more noble sort; those it might expect an Earl to have had better acquaintance with. By the end of my first day of searching I had discovered this line of enquiry was a fruitless one. All my entreaties were firmly rebuffed as soon as it was learned whose agent I was. While my ejections from their homes were more polite than Señora Gonzales' had been, they were just as final.

It appears that being known as an associate of Earl Edgar's is not a badge of great repute amongst those who value such things. Those with the better sort of reputation soon came to avoid him, and despite his death such attitudes still remain. I have assurances the addresses I presented myself to on that first day are those of folk who were known to socialise with the Earl in the earlier days of his residency. It seems now they wish this fact forgotten.

As such, I was forced to focus my investigations upon the lower rungs of the social ladder. On the second day, bracing myself for the rougher environs of the city, I widened my search to the lower reaches; the taverns and public houses that had been noted as Earl Edgar's more frequent haunts.

It was here, at last, that I found those willing to recount tales of their associations with the Earl, for the cost of a drink or two. Many of these tales I find so fanciful that I am sure they have undergone at least a little embellishment for the retelling, but even those of a more believable nature are still wild. They do not tell of the actions one would associate with a peer of the realm.

Yesterday I found myself in a tavern close by the docks where I spoke to a one eyed man who swore to me, on his mother's life no less, that it was the Earl whom had pricked it out in a brawl over a third man's wife. The tale went that the Earl, seeming a demon in drink, had loudly professed his desire to bed a particular lady within that very tavern. The gentlemen told me he informed the Earl that the lady in question was married to a friend of his; a man of good reputation, away fighting in the north of the country. The Earl allegedly flew into a rage at this and took out the man's eye with his knife. For one so wronged, the man seemed to have remarkably little anger towards the Earl for this action, and indeed told me Edgar returned the next morning to ensure he received the best medical care that could be bought. Of the fate of the lady's respectability, he could not recall.

Other such tales I have been told, all in some way adding to the general debasement of the nobility of the Leer name and title. In one hotel I was directed to speak with a serving man who recalled a day when the Earl arrived in the lounge and loudly held forth to the clientele about his sexual conquests in the lands of the far east. Each time one of the horrified patrons fled his candid tirade he would throw a handful of cash from his pocket at the owner to cover the loss.

Many of these tales do not bear repetition, but the collection as a whole depicts Earl Edgar as a man struck by a duality of the soul. He could harangue those he passed in the street with crass obscenities, but could also act the true English gentleman and the very soul of polite expression.

One habit he soon became renowned for was at times to settle at some establishment, call forth for the finest drinks they might serve, be that the richest brandy or the most questionable beer, and then consume all that was brought to him until it seemed his very soul would drown. Inevitably he would be escorted home or thrown out into the street. Neither outcome seemed to bother or dissuade him.

One thing I have made note of in all of this is the lack of reference to the Earl's first wife, Lady Margaret. There are many mentions of the young Maria Juanita, but of Lady Margaret there has been nothing. I can only surmise she must have perished whilst at sea before their arrival at the city. This remains the most frustratingly elusive fact in all my investigations.

Yesterday I struck upon a great piece of luck. I have been introduced to one Carlos Valta, a man who actually served within the Earl's household for a number of years. He had not been in close confidence with the Earl or his new wife, being but a lowly footman, but was nevertheless in an excellent position to view the goings on of the house before the growing disrepute forced him to tender his resignation.

Having been introduced, I arranged to meet with him the next day in one of the nicer salons of the city, which it turned out he in fact owned. A neat, rotund man in his late twenties, Valta spoke a passable English, which was a relief to me as it allowed us to bolster my, thankfully improving, Spanish. I ordered drinks; coffee for myself, while he drank a strange, bitter concoction made from dried leaves called maté, which he drank from a cup and straw, both carved extravagantly from silver. He had a habit of looking around himself as he spoke, never seeming to settle for more than a few moments. Nevertheless his testimony was a welcome enlightenment to the lifestyle of the late Earl.

His story went that he came to Earl Edgar's employ four years ago. By that point the Earl was well established in the town, and those of good standing had already begun their ostracism of him. Valta informed me that he knew well the reputation of his employer, however a position within the household of an Earl still seemed a good prospect for a young man of growing means. Being young and red blooded, he had also felt there might be certain opportunities to be taken advantage of in such a position that would be unavailable in households of a more moral attitude.

Valta told me how he soon discovered the Earl's household was less of an opportunity and more of an endurance. By the time of his employment the better set had already begun to shun the Earl and his young wife, and within their home even the pretence of elegance or morality was long forgotten. He recalled an unsavoury air that made him uncomfortable from the beginning, but he stuck it out for what benefits could be had.

He never knew of the Lady Margaret, nor was the name ever mentioned within his hearing that he could recall. Of the Earl's family, all he knew of was the Lady Maria. It seems the Earl's young wife cared little for the running of her household, and left most of the business that should have been her charge to the servants while she followed her husband's lifestyle. Often, Señor Valta told me, she would wonder around the halls in a state of undress, casually flirting with all she came across. She was unashamed, and openly discussed acts of sexual congress with her visitors while entreating them to the same.

At the start of his employment Valta found such a sight exciting in its shocking brazenness. To his shame, he admits that in those first weeks he gave in to weakness and temptation, allowing the lady to seduce him into actions and behaviours of which he would not speak directly. But being by nature a sober and God fearing man, Señor Valta assures me that despite his healthy, youthful lusts, the behaviours into which he was enticed to indulge did not sit well with him. The Lady Maria's temperament was, he tells me, volatile, and the Earl's even more so. Quickly, Valta began to ensure he was never left alone with his employer's wife and the temptations she presented.

The maids of the household seemed to have been collected from the streets of the city for their talents in areas other than that of housekeeping. Their lack of morality was never a secret, and while they were not as brazen as the lady of the house, visitors were always aware of their nature and the liberties they allowed. Indeed, Señor Valta informed me quite openly the main reason he remained in the Earl's employment for so long were those same liberties. Apparently while he had morals enough to steer away from the Earl's wife, enjoying the company of these common women of low social standing did not hold the same discomfort.

The conversation was one of a strange contrast. He sat before me yesterday in an impeccable suit and sipping through his delicate silver straw, and it was hard to envision him as such a young man as he described. Yet I can think of no reason for him to invent such a testimony, even were it not seemingly corroborated by tales I have collected around the town.

The Earl himself, Señor Valta recalled, was a man prone to bursts of wild emotion or intense self pity. He rarely spoke with the servants, ignoring them completely for the most part. Those occasions he did seek Valta out were usually to berate him for some petty or imagined issue. He seemed to care as little in encountering men he knew had lain with his wife, as he did for how many knew of his own conquests, yet he would fly into obscene rages over the pettiest thing. At times the loss of a small item would send him into a pillar of fury, and once Valta witnessed him violently assault one visitor for turning a corner at the wrong moment and startling him.

In all, Valta spent a little over two years in the Earl's employ, and in that time, he told me, Earl Edgar grew more and more wild, sinking farther into drink and indulging in various opiates. Often he, the Lady Maria and their guests would be found lain out in their rooms insensible. As the years progressed, the Earl retreated more and more into himself as his lifestyle took its inevitable toll on his moods.

In the end, Señor Valta told me, he left the Earl's employ for more mundane reasons than a growing sense of morality. Eventually the maintenance of the household began to break down to such a level that it became a struggle each month for the staff to draw their pay. There came a point where Valta and two of the maids decided the time had come to seek out their fortunes elsewhere. After their engagement and association with Earl Leer they knew their chances of finding similar employment were low, but between them, Valta claims, they had saved enough capitol to invest in the salon in which we now sat. From his demeanour as he told me this, I am left with the impression there may have been more underhand dealing to allow them to leave the Earl's employ with that much money, but such a thing is beyond my remit to investigate. If indeed they did steal that investment capitol,

I cannot judge it any worse than the amounts willingly spent by Earl Edgar on more trivial things. Even if I took an interest in doing so, I doubt I would be able to uncover any proof of theft after this length of time. I also doubt Earl Sebastian would be greatly interested in any case, especially if such actions prolonged the conclusion of my business here.

Señor Valta invited me to dine with him at the salon that night, and indeed meet those two ladies with whom he shared the ownership of the place, but I politely declined his offer. As much as they might have been able to tell me more of the Earl and his household, that which I had already been told had left me feeling distinctly unsettled. Should I fail to discover more information through other sources I might return, but otherwise I was happy to leave that place and return to my own rooms.

But despite my unease, my conversation with Señor Valta has given me much insight into the final years of the Earl's life. The list of sins and evils he sunk to, and those he dragged along with him, makes my stomach turn. I fear for the reaction of Earl Sebastian when I am forced to present my account of his father's life. I hope for my own sake that once this business is over I never again have cause to think on them.

Friday, 19th April 1816

This morning, when I arrived at the coffee shop of Señor Certona where I planned to begin my day, I was immediately hailed by Arthur Cartwright. I had not seen him these last two days. Conspiratorially, he informed me he had succeeded in locating the Lady Maria, and discovered a place and time where we might come upon her unescorted.

He has ascertained that she does indeed live with her

family, her mother a harridan gatekeeper to forever shield her from the outward temptations of sin. Under such guard, the widow has little engagement with the outside world. However, Arthur had ascertained that she visited the local church each day in the morning, often staying there to pray until long past noon. He had watched her and seen this was the only time she would be outside her home unchaperoned. Should I be waiting outside said church, the very one we passed on the end of her street, I could hope for the chance to speak with her alone.

Quickly the two of us repeated our trek to the outskirts of the city. This time I took care to dress less formally than I had for the previous trip, and so felt less conspicuous. There were fewer folk out this morning and while many of them still turned to watch us pass, their gazes did not seem to linger as they had before.

Cartwright brought us through an alternate route so we would not need to walk past the home of that indomitable matron who had thwarted my previous visit, and we went straight to the church at the top of the street. A fair sized building, the edifice was well built of white stone and wood with little adornment other than the large crucifix I had noticed on my previous visit. A small graveyard stood behind, and around the front a sizeable communal garden was kept; a pleasant haven amongst the close-set houses.

Stepping inside, we removed our hats and looked around the interior. It was decorated in the ostentatiously Catholic style, so at odds with my own religious upbringing. Not here the austere walls and plain decoration of the English country church. Instead, painted crucifixes and images of saints surrounded us. To one side stood a rack of candles, and on the alter a large brass crucifix glistened in the low light.

There were two women seated in the pews, far enough apart to indicate that they were not together, their heads bowed in prayer. One was clearly too old to be the one we sought, with a stooped back and strands of white hair showing from underneath a dark veil. The other was young, with long dark brown hair caught up and bound sombrely under her own veil. Though I did not have a view of her face, going by Cartwright's description I was confident we had found the Lady Maria.

Not wanting to disturb her in her prayer, we waited at the back of the church. I felt uncomfortable, as if trespassing on another's secret ritual. I have never been the most avid of church goers, but something about this foreign style of worship strikes me as discomforting. The ostentation of the whole business does not sit right with my nature. I could no more shake the sense of intrusion as I could the rank smell of incense from my nose.

Eventually the younger woman stood, bowed and crossed herself before turning to leave. Upon seeing her face for the first time, I could not help but feel struck by how her actual appearance jarred with the image I had conjured of the woman who had been described to me. She had smooth, olive skin and wide, beautiful eyes filled with a resigned sadness that gave her beauty a poignant edge. Could this woman truly be the degenerate temptress and fornicator of whom I had been told? She was thin; her skin clinging to her cheekbones in such as way that caused me to wonder if she had recently recovered from some illness. She had the appearance of the Romantic heroine. While the face lacked a certain strength, there was an unmistakable pride and determination to her. She seemed older than I knew her years to be, but then a lifestyle of sin and excess is known to age one greatly.

We stood as she approached and I made our introductions. She did not seem surprised at who I was, as if she were expecting my visit. I asked her if she minded speaking to me about her late husband. She seemed reticent, but agreed as long as we did not mind remaining on the church grounds as once she left them she was bound to return to her mother's home. I saw no reason for us not to remain, but with the weather here as humid as it is, combining with my discomfort at those Catholic surroundings, I begged to sit in the churchyard. Nodding, she led us out and around the building to a small bench that sat in the shade against the church wall.

Once we had taken our seats, I explained my reasons for seeking her out. She stared ahead as I did so, saying nothing. She did not react as I informed her of Earl Sebastian's instruction that she and her child be legally disinherited, never to be considered part of the Leer family. She seemed to have been expecting such a judgment, and gave no indication of how such news affected her. Truth be told, I believe I was the most shaken of the three of us. The image of our little group sitting there in the shade of that foreign church as I explained to her that her child would never be considered the equal of his half brother, shall forever be etched in my memory.

As I finished, she simply sat in silence. I had expected something more; some supplication for clemency, for money or aid for her and her son. She did not even mention him. After a moment she turned to me and asked if there was anything else I required. I admit I felt more than wretched. I had just conveyed to her the damnation of her prospects, and here I was asking her to aid me in my chronicling of her clearly unmourned husband's final years. I felt uncomfortable enough as it was, bringing up such tales on church grounds. I am glad Mr. Cartwright had been there, or else the inappropriateness of the situation may have gotten the better of me.

The Lady Maria looked to the sky, and began to pray in a

low, mumbled Spanish. I could just about follow her, but her prayers did not seem specific. She looked back at me, and told me she would answer what questions I had. She told me that God required her penance, and if she was to be absolved of her many sins then she must face that which she had done, and pray for His mercy.

As she told her story she never once showed any emotion. Her recitation was blank and flat, as if these facts were something she had gone over again and again until they had lost all meaning. She spoke as if they were something from another life. When I had a question, she would respond, and I believe the only times she omitted any details were to spare my own obvious blushes. At times both myself and Mr. Cartwright became quite uncomfortable as this woman of such delicate appearance recounted some of the things she and the Earl had experienced. She herself seemed little affected, and showed no embarrassment at speaking so to two strangers.

I will account here the bare bones of her tale, for I have no wish to repeat it in such details as she was prepared to offer.

Maria met the Earl within a few weeks of his arrival in the city. She was a maid in one of the many public houses. The name of the establishment was not one I have visited in my short time, but she was unabashed about neither its reputation, or her part in the same. She was, by her own admission, a lady of what can only be politely described as low morals. While not yet sunk so low as the Earl's association would take her, she would intersperse serving tables with drinking and gambling with those she served, and saw little shame in flirting with those patrons who could provide her with the opportunity for such things. But she was young and beautiful, and one of those whose gifts in that direction leave them little thought for their eventual chances of salvation.

It was at this time that she met Earl Edgar. Apparently he took quickly to the young, debauched serving girl. The evening they met, the Earl was in one of the lavish moods he later became known for, and the next morning found many of the clientèle, including the young Maria, waking in his apartments.

There was no sign of the Lady Margaret at this point, and Maria recalled that the Earl neither mentioned her nor acted as one recently widowed. In this I am forced to conclude that the Earl's first wife died sometime on his final voyage. It vexes me that I cannot find more concrete information for the family chronicles. Maria, in fact, claims she did not learn of the Earl's first wife until well after they were married, an event that happened very soon after their first meeting. She had quickly become a favourite of his, and he of hers. He was rich and poured extravagancies on her, and she, I blush to tell, assures me she was just as free with her affections towards him. When the Earl insisted upon their marriage, Maria was eager to ensure the lifetime of luxury that she believed it would entail and saw no reason to question his rash decision.

It strikes me as odd that the Earl should wish to marry so soon after the death of his wife. From his reputation, he does not strike me as one who would feel any moral compunctions towards keeping a mistress, even in the public eye. I know from the Lady Maria's own admission, corroborated by the other accounts I have heard, that neither she nor the Earl considered the blessed state of monogamy as part of their lives. Why they bothered with the ritual at all I cannot say, but Edgar was insistent she be his wife, and so his wife she became. Upon this abrupt marriage her family, already displeased with their daughter's reputation, disowned her for a whore. At the time, she told us, this was an act that concerned her little. She had a rich husband and a life of luxury. Why should she care for the opinions of those who judged her.

I shall spare in this writing the accounts she gave of her life with the Earl. Suffice it to say she admits the tales and reputation that have been lain upon her name across the city are more than truthful. She drank, fornicated, cheated, lied, partook of narcotics and otherwise lived a life of decadence and devilry. This she readily admitted, all in that flat, emotionless voice. It is, she explained, why she now spends what life she has remaining in prayer and repentance for those sins.

Eager to move on from such topics, I urged the lady to recount the last days of the Earl's life, so that I might have that which I came for and be on my way. I consider myself a man of the world and well aware of its temptations and vulgarities. I did not spend my own youth cloistered as a monk, and have sampled the temptations life has offered as much as any young man. But the casual manner in which this woman recounted all that she had undertaken in her short life truly shook me.

The first four years of her marriage continued much in the same vein. However, in the last two years of his life the Earl began to show signs of the madness that gradually grew to consume him. Maria, and all those who knew him, had always been aware of his temper. The rages he would fly into over the smallest thing were famous, but they began to occur more and more frequently. Also, in the last year of his life, he began to both drink and consume opiates at an alarming rate. He grew more and more withdrawn from the world, and those who had been prepared to stay around him for the excesses he offered began to fall away. He left his apartments less and less, leaving off his toilet and appearing unshaven and poorly dressed.

By this time Maria had given birth to her son, a child she

named Tobias. It is for the best that Earl Sebastian has already decided to formally disown the child from the family. For all Maria insists there is no doubt the child is Edgar's, she readily admits to regular infidelities. From the lifestyle and immorality she described of herself, any reasonable man would be sceptical of a claim of paternity.

Whatever the parentage, the birth of Tobias seemed to have some effect on both mother and supposed father. Maria claims the pangs of childbirth calmed something within her. The Earl, on the other hand, cut himself off from mother and child completely, muttering vagaries about strange curses and unnatural blood whenever they were mentioned in his presence.

It seems clear to me that at this point his mind had begun to give way to whatever wasting disease was to take him. Maria told us how, in those final weeks, Edgar would drink constantly; never abating, always seeming to require more. And yet she insists that during this period he was the most sober she can recall him in the whole of their marriage. Despite all he would imbibe it seemed he could not become intoxicated. His paranoia grew, and he would scream at anyone who came close. He shouted wild accusations of stalkers hounding him, insisting he was being followed everywhere, even when he was locked away alone. Eventually he stopped eating altogether, and rapidly grew emaciated until his appearance was skeletal and gaunt. The few times Maria saw him in those last weeks, he was little more than a spectre of a man.

By that time, the lady Maria found her life had collapsed around her and become a living hell. Without a husband in his right mind, their financial capital soon ran dry. As the servants abandoned them she was effectively living in lavish poverty. Edgar would fly into a rage if she or her son even approached, and she lived out those last days hidden and unattended in her rooms. It was then, she told us, that she began to recognise and reflect on the evil life she had brought her son into.

For the last month of his life, Earl Edgar locked himself away in his rooms and would allow no one access. Other than the occasional exclamation of anger or fear he made no attempt at communication with the outside world. By this time only two of their servants remained, mostly out of pity for the wretched girl their mistress had become, but they made no attempts at reaching the Earl. It was not until bailiffs came to the house that his rooms were broken into and his corpse discovered.

It was here, for the first time, that Maria seemed hesitant to speak. For all she had already told us, things that would make the worst of soldiers blush, this one event caused her to hold back.

She described to us the scene that had been unveiled when the bailiffs had led her into Edgar's rooms. The whole of the apartment had been smashed and broken, as if the late Earl had been in some great rage. There were papers strewn all about, covered in almost incomprehensible writings. A fire had been lit in the middle of the floor, now a pile of cold ashes with soot staining the ceiling above. The Earl's body was huddled in the corner. It had been skeletal, she told us; its skin pale and thin, clinging to his bones. The men there had at first refused to believe the body had been there only a month, for though lacking much decomposition it had the appearance and condition of having been dead far longer.

Two things Maria told us that had stuck in her mind before she had been forced to flee the room. The first was the smell. One would think such a thing to be expected in the self imposed tomb of a diseased madman, but Maria insisted the air did not hold the stench of death or decay, but a dry smell; a musty odour that seemed alien to the muggy confines of the room.

The second was the look of pure terror on Edgar's face. Her speech stumbled here, as if the recollection were still too fresh. She began to describe it, but seemed unable to bring herself to do so. I imagine that in the state her mind must have been in at the time, seeing her husband in death must have been too much for her constitution. I cannot say I blame her.

Now we had come to the end of Maria's story. She told how those few possessions of value she still held were all taken to provide for the debts Edgar had accrued. In his madness it had been long since he had sent for money from England, and quickly she found herself and her son with nothing but a few items of clothing remaining them. She and the Earl had retained few friends in the city, and there was no good favour to her name. Maria had been left with little choice but to return to her family and beg for their charity. This they had given, with the frosty and rigid redemption of Catholics.

Now I had heard this tale, her mother's reception to me, an agent of the Earl's family, became clear. Having managed to pull her disgraced daughter back from damnation, she wished to keep her from all harbingers of temptation that might appear to drag back from the brink of redemption.

It was, by this time, well into the afternoon and I was eager for this uncomfortable conversation to come to a close. I thanked Maria and stood to take my leave. Before we left, Arthur asked her about the sheets of writing she had mentioned which had been found in the late Earl's apartments. I am grateful for his presence, for shaken as I felt I had not even thought to enquire. These artefacts from the final days of the Earl's life would have to be recovered, if only to demonstrate the state of the Earl's mind. That some wasting disease took his sanity I am now absolutely certain, and a sample of these ravings in his hand would be the proof required to show it.

Maria told us they, along with a few other items of an equal dearth of value, were returned to her once creditors had stripped her of what possessions still remained; mostly papers and documents that had survived the Earl's madness and decline. Upon our urging, she told us she had never read them but had yet to rid herself of them either. They remained still in her family home, packed away in remembrance.

Seeing the need to recover the Earl's last thoughts, whatever madness they may show, and to do some little charity for this poor woman, I offered payment for the recovery of the notes. Still she regarded me blankly, but I thought perhaps I saw some glimmer of emotion in her eyes as she agreed to accept my naked offer of aid; some deep acknowledgement of my pity, and a thankfulness for it. Or perhaps I simply saw what I wished to see; some sign of humanity in this fallen woman. Some indication that even one who had sinned so fully and absolutely could find redemption. In either case she agreed to bring the documents with her tomorrow when she came to pray. It would be impossible for her to do so today without her mother enquiring into her purpose.

With that, we thanked her and gratefully took our leave. The air, still so humid and close, had taken on a sickly edge. How could such a wretched creature bear such a fragile beauty? Arthur and I spoke little on the walk back to my lodgings. My mind was filled with horror and fascination at the life to which the late Earl had sunk. All the rumours I had collected were now confirmed by his widow and companion in debauchery. I did, and still do, feel truly shaken at that which I learned today.

Saturday, 20th April 1816

I slept badly last night. The weather has become even closer. Twice it forced me from my bed to stand at the open window, vainly seeking some slight breeze to alleviate the heat. My shirt clings to my frame. The air outside is as still as death and I can find no relief from the humidity.

Arthur arrived this morning, as we had arranged, but I begged off accompanying him. I put the payment I intended for the widow in his hands and asked that he might make the visit alone, for lack of sleep and the oppressive atmosphere have robbed me of my vitality and I felt in no mood to travel far.

Cartwright, good fellow that he is, readily agreed. Indeed, he commented on my complexion and asked if I required anything that might aid my constitution. I assured him I simply needed the rest that was denied me last night, along with some respite from this infernal weather.

Having passed on the task, I will attempt now to regain some sleep. Maybe then I shall have the strength to travel to the coffee shop and take in some air.

Sunday, 21st April 1816

He haunts me. While I am awake, the walls seem to close in upon me. Even in sleep I am granted no respite from the torments on my mind. The tunnel. I see the tunnel that goes on, and the endless darkness that waits beyond. I feel I have entered that darkness before, yet I have no memory of the place. The eyes. Following. Watching each and every step along this predestined and chaotic roadway. I am scared. Terrified of what I found within. I have no recollection of this place, yet I am no stranger to it. For all I have never been here before, in this life or any other, I know it. I know it too well. What did I find within? Are these truly my memories? Someone watches me. I know them, yet I do not know them. I cannot escape it.

Friday, 27th April 1816

I have no memory of making that last entry.

This last week I have been struck down by a local malady, one I have been told often passes through the town in the late days of summer. The fever broke only yesterday, and I am assured I am now past the worst danger. By Señor Mercallo's account it is a common thing in these parts and none but the most infirm have any real fear from it. I cannot say I am convinced by this, for it has drained me of all strength and vigour. I can think and I can write, but any pursuits that require more than the slightest physical application are beyond me. Today the simple act of dressing myself has left me weak and breathless.

My salvation and saviour has been the redoubtable Arthur Cartwright. When he returned last Saturday afternoon with the documents he had retrieved from the widow Maria I was not, as we had arranged, waiting at Señor Certona's coffee house. Coming to my apartments, he could get no answer from knocking upon my door. He left then, assuming I was detained upon some errand. Yet when he returned the following morning to find I was still unreachable, and knowing how I had wished to acquire those papers with all haste, he became worried. Seeking out my landlord he entreated Señor Mercallo to unbar my door with his own key. There I was found, laid out upon the floor.

I was quickly brought down to the Mercallo's own rooms, where the family have nursed me through the illness. For this kindness, and Cartwright's diligence, I am eternally grateful. I have no others in this city I might have fallen upon in such a time, and they bore no obligation to watch over me as they have.

As weak as I am, I am assured that now the fever has broken I am in no lasting danger, but must simply rebuild my strength. The indomitable Señora Mercallo has set it upon herself to see to my convalescence. While she has finally judged me recovered enough to return to my own room, I am still fetched down for each meal of the day. These consist of plates piled high with food, to be taken under her domineering gaze. The strict matron seems willing to force feed me if I do not eat at the required speed. I am grateful to her for her kindness, but her style of nursing is most akin to making me aware she will simply not permit me to become sick again.

I wonder, are all women of this country so strong willed and domineering? I believe I am yet to meet one I could readily describe as demure or unassuming. Is it the climate, or possibly the breeding that makes them so different from an English lady? While those women of my own family are no wilting flowers when it comes to expressing an opinion, none have the same aggressive force of personality I have encountered here.

Today was the first time I have felt the strength or inclination to open this journal, and am shocked to discover the previous entry; dated Sunday the twenty-first. I have no memory of writing it. Though there can be no doubt the words are written in my hand, I would readily swear that I had never seen those words before today. I can only imagine that I scribed them whilst in some nightmare; a delirium brought about by my sickness. While I have no recollection of such a dream, or anything of that day, reading the words back now does strike some chord within me. Some echo of memory convinces me it was I who wrote the words. Reading them over leave me with an unsavoury sense of unease. I am glad I cannot recall whatever nightmare inspired them.

I am despondent my work is now delayed by this illness, but I thank providence that it was not so much worse. As weak as it has left me, I cannot yet hope to begin again with my tasks. Even should I try, I am sure Señora Mercallo would not allow such exertion. The notes Arthur brought sit unread upon my desk. Hopefully by the beginning of the week I will have regained enough of my strength to resume my business.

Monday, 29th April 1816

My condition has improved much over the weekend. Señora Mercallo's stringent nursing has aided the recovery of my strength to the point where I feel almost my old self, though my clothing hangs loose on a frame that is notably slimmer than it once was.

The humidity is still yet to break. Sleep remains uncomfortable and troubled, though not so much as before my illness. Yet this morning I awoke refreshed enough to venture once more out into the world.

My first undertaking was to travel to the home of Arthur Cartwright to thank him most profoundly for his assistance. Not only has he been an invaluable aid to me in my business about the city, but without him I cannot say whether I would even be alive. In my weakened state, I may well have remained undiscovered until the illness had fully taken me. That this redoubtable Welshman took it upon himself, those years ago, to settle here in Argentina is something for which I shall forever be thankful. I insisted upon taking him out to lunch, and feted him with the best dining rooms I could entice him to name. We dined well. My convalescence has given me appetite far greater than usual, and through this his own was encouraged to greater excess.

This afternoon, merry from our meal and in good spirits all round, I retired to the coffee shop of Señor Certona. Earl Edgar's notes still await me in my rooms, but I feel too well with the world to begin sifting through the final words of a sinful madman. I have managed to acquire an English newspaper from one of the latest ships to arrive in port, and for a time I am content to read of my own England. Later I shall search out a gift of some kind for Señora Mercallo, in grateful thanks for her nursing.

Tomorrow I shall begin my work. For now, I shall enjoy my health.

Tuesday, 30th April 1816

My mind is troubled.

Today I sat down to the task of sorting through the notes that were reclaimed from Lady Maria. I had expected a few sheets, nothing more. The folder Mr. Cartwright purchased from Maria, which she in turn inherited from her late husband's meagre estate, contains perhaps up to seventy pages of scrawled ramblings. With no clear order that I can discern, the ink-stained and crumpled pages that now stare up at me from the floor of my room seem to provide nothing but riddles.

At first I had hoped that once I began I might come across some clear pattern or narrative thrust on which to order the pages. In this I was disappointed. There appears to be little enough connection between each line. At least none I can ascertain. Often a sheet will have several different amendments, seemingly added at different times. Some are crumpled, as if discarded then retrieved and reused. Some of the ink has been smudged at the time of writing, and to a greater extent than one might expect from simply careless penmanship. It is almost as if the author did not wish to see his own words. Many of the pages are burned; either with intent or perhaps the Earl was simply careless of the damage. There is a great variety in severity, with some pages badly charred and missing sections while others are merely singed. The widow did mention the remains of a fire in his rooms. I wonder whether there were many more pages that did not survive that might have garnered greater enlightenment to the rest?

My best guess is that with the wasting disease taking his mind, Edgar was perhaps attempting to make sense of his disjointed thoughts. To stare down at this outpouring from a dying mind fills me with unease. It seems almost enough to send one to bedlam itself. It is like I am witness to his last days, his final thoughts. His collapse into mania and death.

Perhaps I am putting too much thought into this. Is my desire to seek out meaning in a madman's words leading me to search for that which does not exist? Yet if I could finalise and resolve this before my return I can only believe that Misters Caine and Dennings would greater see my suitability for advancement within the firm. I fully admit that while many sensible men would discard these pages, my ambition drives me to do more.

Upon discovering the random nature of the notes, I made some attempt at cataloguing what I read so I might discover some system or cypher that could aid me. I was soon forced to abandon this plan. The topics chop and change with no apparent pattern or structure. From some I can ascertain a vague meaning while others offer only chaotic gibberish.

Some things do perhaps shed a little light on heretofore unlit points in the narrative I seek. On one page can clearly be read the words *"Into the sea she went, unable to face that which would come. Poor Margaret. She never wished it, but still it comes to us. Perhaps she was more in the right than I, that in foolishness I stood to fight it still. Perhaps I am stronger, or perhaps I was the coward. I know her in the dark. The tunnel, she is there. Oh..."* The rest of the line is lost where a hand has clearly smudged the words to illegibility.

I feel there can be no doubt this paragraph refers to Lady Margaret, the Earl's first wife. *"Into the sea"* can clearly be interpreted as indication that she died on their voyages. The more sinister reading might infer than she in fact took her own life. Is it possible? That she shared her husband's reputation as much as the Lady Maria later did is well known. I cannot deny the possibility that, beset by a sudden remorse for her sinful life, she might undertake such an act. But what is this that he refers to as *"that which would come"*? Perhaps he refers to the final illness that took his own mind. Mayhap the pair knew of their contagion, and Lady Margaret could not endure the knowledge of the suffering and madness that awaited them? Or perhaps it took her far sooner than he?

This page is one of the few to focus only on one topic. Where the ink has not been wiped and smeared, the surviving letters contain a number of other references to his late wife. *"Margaret Maria. Margaret. Maria. It will not be distracted. So alike, yet the focus lies upon me"* is one, and *"Over her shoulder he lurks. He has Margaret, I know it, but he shall have me! Have me! Us! Me!"*

Perhaps, in his last days, the Earl's mind began to find difficulty differentiating between his two wives. At times their two names seem interchanged, at other points they are clearly seen as separate people. Another, regrettably undamaged, page seems to consist of nothing but accounts of lurid acts of sexual congress with both women. Written in a tiny, cramped hand across both sides of the sheet, the lines merge and run over each other as if written in some sort of frenzy. What incited him to write such things is beyond me. Other pages also make mention of these acts, but I shall not repeat them here.

There is one page that refers unquestionably to Edgar's father, the Earl Andrew who died with *The Endeavour*. It first drew my eye as it seems to be one of the longest uninterrupted phrases in this entire macabre collection. I shall recreate it here now:

So little did father know. Oh Andrew, Earl Andrew and foolish mother. All alone and the son so far away. No idea could he have had what all at once lay within Endeavour. So evil, so dark. Nor did I, did I know who what it was. No indeed. I should not have searched it, no. Ptalantohtep did not wish it, and now I am followed. Foolish. Foolish. Cursed cargo such things forgotten for so long. Why me why her? Others maybe. How many?

Here at the end there looks to have once been more, but the lower portion of the page is burned away, and this is all that remains upon the unburned fragment that can be deciphered. It clearly demonstrates that Edgar had some knowledge about his parent's final voyage. I know little of the trip myself, aside from the fact they had been sailing from their estates in Ireland to Portsmouth and that the ship was taken in a storm. The name Ptalantohtep is a mystery to me, if indeed it is a name. So untidy and rushed is the writing, it is hard enough to read that I might well be mistaken. What I record here is the closest facsimile I can ascertain.

As I write the word a strange feeling comes over me. Indeed it seems to have been growing as I have continued to read these pages. I have no doubt the final words of a madman could have this effect on any man. Thoughts and questions fill my head. I must rest, lest this mood overtake me. I am simply weak from the illness. Such immersion must be overcoming me. I shall continue tomorrow.

Wednesday, 1ˢᵗ May 1816

Last night I found only a fitful slumber. I spent the preceding evening in a local tavern. I sat alone, seeking some respite from the oppressive heat. I was unable to drag my mind away from those macabre pages. Images of crazed and haphazard writing floated before my eyes. When I returned to my apartment, sleep alluded me.

Today I continued my research on Edgar's notes. Discarding the majority of the more illegible pages, I took a sample to the coffee shop and sat poring over them once more, attempting to find some pattern or theme. My mind keeps returning to that one passage regarding Edgar's father. Of all the obscene, mysterious ramblings, this one page haunts me most. I wish I knew more about the late Earl Andrew's final voyage, but there is little I can do to discover more here. All I can imagine is Earl Edgar discovered some piece of information regarding that fateful trip that had heretofore gone undiscovered. I cannot help but wonder on this evil he mentions. Once I return home I might be able to discover more. For now, as much as I tell myself such speculation is less than idle, I cannot dismiss it.

And the name; Ptalantohtep. It has the sound of the Egyptian. Earl Edgar travelled much in his life, and I know he visited the African continent on various occasions. It certainly does not have a modern sound, yet the excerpt speaks as if of something alive.

I fear I am seeking too deep for meaning in these missives. Any sane man would agree they are little more than ravings, with no import other than proof that Edgar's mind had gone. I would destroy the pages in the hope of freeing myself from this fascination were it not for the fact that I must return them to England to be included in the family archives. Be they simple ravings or something deeper, they are still the last artefacts of the eleventh Earl Leer, and must be recorded.

Despite my work these last two days I have found no trick or pattern that might unlock any meaning from Edgar's notes. I must accept that there is almost certainly nothing to find. While the mystery continues to pull at my thoughts I cannot help but think the ravings are only serving to further my discomfort. I have bound them well within a thick leather pouch ready for transport back to England, together with the reports and certificates I have gathered. I have little more than a week remaining before my return voyage, and must not allow myself to become obsessed with this fool's errand.

Saturday, 4th May 1816

How I wish for my ship to dock. The climate of Buenos Aires has become near enough unbearable; the heat and humidity too much for my British constitution. Even though I show no more signs of my former illness, still I am denied the elixir of a full night's sleep. Since the fever I have been beset with strange nightmares. I can recall nothing solid of them, but their half imagined horrors have kept my mind from any restful slumber. Each time I come close to sleep I find myself thrown from rest once more by that which awaits me.

While my nights are filled with these subtle fears, my days have taken on shades of discomforting supposition. I have begun to find I cannot shake a feeling that someone follows me. Each time I venture out into the city I swear I feel eyes upon me, following me as I am about my appointments. I have been able to find no trace of any such tail, but still the feeling persists. I have asked Señors Mercallo and Certona if any have asked after me, but they both assure me otherwise.

Last night I met again with Arthur Cartwright and confided to him my concerns. He dismissed them goodheartedly. He assures me my discomfort comes from the unseasonal heat, and I am simply unused to it. There is no wonder, he tells me, that it affects my sleep. He suffered in exactly the same manner in his first year here, and it often takes visitors so. With the late summer holding on as it has, there is little that can be done other than seeking what comforts I may.

Oh, how I pray for the dry, gentle warmth of an English summer!

Monday, 6th May 1816

Yesterday I went to church. It is something I have not done since my arrival here, yet after this last week I felt a need for a little sanctity.

Last night, more than once, I felt certain some other presence hovered in the room with me; some spectre from my dreams made manifest. There was none there but myself of course but numerous times I awoke and, irrational as it may have been, was compelled each time to leave my bed to look about my room. Once done, I would then begin my quest for slumber afresh.

I did not seek out an Anglican church, should there even be one in this town, but simply visited the one nearest my apartments. The Catholic rites were foreign to my sensibilities, and I am sure that should my mother ever learn I sat through such a Papist ceremony she would find great cause to berate me. I sat at the back of the building, surrounded by the soberly clad city folk, while the Latin and the stench of incense swirled around us and I prayed for some hope of salvation from my troubles.

Whatever sanctity the church might have offered, however, has not delivered any lasting abatement of my unease. Though during the service itself I was but one of a crowd and felt a fresh and pleasing anonymity, once I had taken myself outside to the street the oppressive heat and suspicious eyes once again fell upon me.

Perhaps Cartwright is correct. Maybe I am simply feeling this foreign summer. With my mind curtailed by the lack of sleep my thoughts are not as they should be. I am finding it harder to concentrate. At least I feel my mission here in Buenos Aires has been completed to a degree that will reflect well on me, if not so cleanly as I would have liked. Perhaps with my involvement in this shameless chapter of the Leer family history over, and once I am returned to my native shore, my mind might at last find the peace it has been missing.

Tuesday, 7th May 1816

Last night I dreamt of Earl Edgar.

His face was clouded and the features unclear, yet I knew it to be him. The widow Maria stood at his side, younger and more fulsome than she had been when I met her at the church. Here was the wanton girl of whom I have been told, with the wicked smile and challenging eyes one would imagine of the girl of her reputation. Behind her was another woman, similar in appearance though years older. She looked of an age with the Earl. There were others there, though less distinct than these three; Arthur Cartwright was one, as was each member of the Mercallo family. I saw my parents, and my poor brother as he was, full of the youth the polio took from him.

There were others still, but most were indistinct as if

standing in a thick black mist. Through the cloud a dark and shadowy figure stalked, prowling between the people before me and examining each in turn. On completing its circuit it came to stand before me. It was nothing but shadow and air, yet I felt its eyes on me. All of a sudden, the black mist burnt away in a dark, consuming flash, as if the day of reckoning had come. Only he and I remained, his eyes burning into me.

I awoke coated with sweat, and with such a pounding in my head that I feared the fever had taken me again. The images did not fade as dreams are want to do, but remained in my mind as clear as memory. My room was stifling with the oppressive heat, so I stumbled from my bed and threw open the windows to the morning. Alas, the air was still as death and brought scarce refreshment. In desperation, for I felt as if the unquenched heat might overcome me, I took the pitcher of water that stands in my room and threw it over my head. Only then did the panic leave me, washed away by the lukewarm liquid that dripped from my face onto the floorboards.

Such a dream I have not had since my childhood. Unlike the half formed visions that have plagued me each night since I have recovered from the fever, this nightmare was as clear in my mind as though the figures I had seen had been here in the flesh. It left me as weak as a babe. For the next hour I could do nothing but sit, waiting for my wits to return.

I now have no wonder why Earl Sebastian wishes the business of his late and unlamented father dealt with and forgotten. I fear my mind is poisoned by the unholy and immoral things I have been forced to uncover since beginning my task. If this is the effect sexamining the late Earl's life and actions has upon a man, then I shall be pleased and grateful to be done with it. I know I shall not sleep well again until the whole damned business is concluded.

Merely three days remain until my ship docks. The sooner

I can pass on all I have to Mr. Dennings the better. Maybe then I can at last be free of it.

Wednesday, 8ᵗʰ May 1816

I am now determined on wrapping up my business in the city with as much haste as possible. I have resolved that I have spent too long in aimless introspection, and that it does my mind no good. I shall busy myself, while I wait for my ship to arrive, by ensuring my work is completed to the required standards. Consigning the folder containing Edgar's final ravings to the bottom of my trunk, I spent the morning sorting those other reports I have gathered. I have read and rewritten all that I have discovered in regards to the Earl's death, and have sorted and bound together all the copies of the documents in my possession. I am confident that I can ensure that there shall be no loose ends remaining.

Despite my baser fears, when I took to my bed last night I was no longer assailed by my previous dreams. I have had my first clear night's sleep since the fever took me. Perhaps I am at last beginning to acclimatise to this foreign weather, though the heat and humidity have still not broken. During the day it is almost unbearable to remain inside, and only marginally improved at night.

Having arranged my work to my satisfaction I took myself upon a walk near the docks, hoping that perhaps a good breeze might avail me. It did, somewhat, but as I walked the feeling of my being followed returned. There are so many eyes in the town that follow me that I cannot ever catch one single individual. Do I stick out so much as a foreigner on these shores? Or has my investigation brought about this unwanted attention? Does someone within the city wish to know who I speak with and where I go? Or perhaps simply to know when I intend to leave? Such speculation is foolish, I know, yet I cannot seem to shake it from my mind.

Thursday, 9th May 1816

This morning I returned to the docks. Despite the eyes on my back, this is the best place to have a hope of finding any breeze to cut the heavy air. And, whilst sitting and staring out across the river, I saw a sight that boosted my spirits in a way I cannot adequately describe. I had been idly watching a ship pull in when I saw the name *April Mercy* upon its prow. My heart was struck with a leap of joy so strong that I let out an exclamation. For this ship is the harbinger of my escape! In two days it is engaged to return me home.

I sat and watched the majestic edifice settle into its mooring. Immediately sailors began to bustle to and fro whilst dockhands swarmed around with nets and cranes. The ship soon began to divulge its cargo of passengers, while swings and pulleys were moved into place to divest the heavier stock. I know little of ships or their ways, and know not the correct terms and expressions for the work or apparatus I saw in use. Yet for the whole afternoon I felt an effusive joy in the sight of maritime business, so that for a time the weather and my nightmares were forgotten.

Having watched the disembarkation of the *April Mercy* until evening began to settle, I made my way quickly to the house of Arthur Cartwright to celebrate my impending liberation from this stifling city and to make a proper goodbye. Arthur has become a firm friend of mine during my stay. He has not only been of invaluable assistance to me in my business here, but also stood forth as the agent of my salvation on that day I was struck with the fever. All apart from this, he also is a pleasant fellow and good company. I have enjoyed the evenings we have spent together, and I feel that of all my memories of this place, it is mainly this time that I shall miss. While, after my experience here, I no longer harbour thoughts of setting myself up within the firm as a liaison with any business in this fledgling country, should the events of my future direct me here again I should not be so unwilling, if it should allow me to be reunited with Arthur Cartwright.

The night has gone long, and it is now well into the morning. Still, my excitement about my impending escape combines with the heat and makes sleep elusive. I have sat up, writing by lamp light in order to calm my mind, but to little avail. I will attempt sleep, though I have pitiful hope of rest.

Friday, 10th May 1816

I awoke this morning feeling notably unwell. While last night's wine had aided me in finding sleep despite the continual heat, this morning they combined to mark a sharp increase in my discomfort. It was almost noon before I was well enough to rouse myself and complete my packing.

I am now set for my return journey; my work filed and cases packed. Tomorrow I shall have everything taken down to the docks early, that they might be packed aboard the *April Mercy*. While this city is indeed a fine place, I am passed eager to be gone. I miss my own climate and am still haunted by whatever presence follows me.

Earlier in the afternoon I took a break from my work and ventured out one last time to Pascal de Certona's coffee shop. I have spent many fine hours there and wished to say a proper goodbye. He was as effusive as ever, and I find I shall miss my time spent at his tables. Upon returning, however, I could not shake the impression that someone had been in my room whilst I was absent. While I could not determine that any of my carefully packed belongings had been disturbed, there was an unsettling certainty within my mind that my things were not exactly as I left them. I enquired with Señora Mercallo, for only she, her husband and I had access to a key to my room, whether any one had visited while I had been out. She assured me no-one had, but despite all possible evidence, the feeling persists.

But I shall forget such foolish worries. Tonight I shall dine with my landlord and his family. I owe Señor Mercallo and his wife much for their nursing of me through my ailment, and they have been most gracious as hosts. Without them my sojourn in this land would have been so much more unpleasant, and I wish to thank them for it.

Saturday, 11th May 1816

At last, I am away.

I write this entry sitting in my cabin aboard the *April Mercy*. It is a small room which I shall be sharing with one other passenger. He is yet to board, so for now I have the space to myself. Though with so much activity around this ship as it prepares to leave, with men moving and shifting cargo and the other passengers finding their accommodation, it is impossible to feel completely alone.

This cabin is a mean room to be spending the coming months in, but I am in such good spirits I cannot bring myself to dwell on such things. My belongings are stowed and I now simply await the evening tide to begin my journey home!

I shall not say that my first voyages abroad have been wholly unpleasant, but still I am eager to be away. While the majority of the people of this city are pleasant, the climate has proven beyond my sensibilities to endure. Despite constant assurances that this is autumn, the weather today seems even warmer still. While my clothing sticks to me and the oppressive humidity holds down my spirit, those others I pass in the street seem almost unaffected. It seems I lack the stamina for this climate.

But soon to sweet England once more. Rather than waiting within the confines of my cabin, I shall see if I can find a spot on deck to take one last look upon this city.

Sunday, 12th May 1816

With the weather having been so still for so long, I had feared that our voyage would be slow. However, once we had passed out of the river and into the open sea we were met with strong, clean winds that had been so absent from the city. I could feel the ship's speed pick up and can only wonder how different these last weeks may have been if only this air had found its way over Buenos Aires.

I have spent this morning on the deck, revelling in the freedoms of the ocean. I had almost forgotten how good it is to have the wind blow against my face, sweeping away the smells and sensations of the last month as the horizon spreads out around me. I have not felt so good in a long while. As I stood out there, the ship rising and falling, the spray misting the air, I found myself laughing. Some of those around me may have looked oddly on me as I did so, but I could not find it within myself to care. The crew may stare as they pass behind me, but I do not mind. My behaviour must seem strange to those used to the freedom of sea travel. They cannot understand how much my soul yearned to be released from that enclosing city.

Monday, 12th May 1816

The weather continues to provide strong winds. As they build, so the sea grows steadily rougher, though not to any alarming degree. I can recall it being much the same on my previous voyage. I am not worried, for I did not suffer from any sickness on the outward voyage and do not fear anything on my return.

I do find that the lack of activity begins to bear upon me. It seems strange to have so much idle time. I realise now I could have spent more of my time in the city at leisure, and saved some of my work to occupy me now. I have no reason to continue writing. This journal was in truth only begun as a way for me to keep notes as I worked, and not intended as a personal record of any kind. Now I find I resort to making further entries simply to occupy my mind. I must take steps to ensure I can remain busy.

My cabin-mate is a likeable enough chap; one Phillip Doungan. He is a man of few words, though has a pleasant demeanour that makes him amiable company. He too is an Englishman who has been in Buenos Aires on business, though for a far longer time than I. He is quiet, and keeps to himself. He does not seem to be comfortable with travel. While I have spent much of my time above decks, he has been mostly confined to his cot. I am sure that we shall grow better acquainted in the coming weeks.

Thursday, 16th May 1816

We have encountered our first storm.

The winds we had been blessed with since leaving Buenos Aires had been building steadily since our journey began.

While I had praised them for the speed which they granted us, by Tuesday evening even I could tell that they had grown dangerous. The seas had become rough and unsettled, and the heaving of the waves caused the ship to creak and fall alarmingly. Soon enough we were all ushered below decks by the crew as they began rushing to prepare the ship for the coming tempest. Phillip Doungan and I sat in our cabin. We spoke little. He, of course, had been feeling unwell since our journey began, and with our cabin tilting and falling around us I had little conversation that could distract the poor man.

The storm hit us full force in the night. I found it hard to sleep, as the ships movements were so rough that comfort was impossible to find. Every so often I would feel Doungan's eyes on me, but the few times I had the strength to raise my head to meet his gaze he would be back huddled on his own bunk.

At some point I must have managed to fall asleep, as I woke later that morning to the sound of the ship's timbers shrieking against the strain of the storm. I do not know how the sailors endured it. During a lull I braved the deck, seeking some escape from the tormented confines of our small cabin. The sky was thick with dark clouds that hung so low they seemed to brush the mast. Cold, harsh spray stung my face and I was forced to retreat below once again.

The storm lasted the entire day, but by yesterday evening the winds finally began to die down. While the sea is still choppy and uneven and the ship rolls alarmingly, compared to the violence we have already endured all seems comparatively serene. I have found a sheltered spot here on deck to use this journal as an escape from the sharp scent of fear and bile that permeates the living spaces below. What I record does not matter overmuch, I simply seek a way to distract my mind.

Friday, 17th May 1816

The weather continues calm. The storm seems to have passed, and we sail cleanly through the South Atlantic. The wind remains strong and part of me fears it is building again, but it does mean we are once again making good speed. It is the strange balance mankind has with nature; harnessing it for our needs and yet helpless to its greater power.

Mr. Doungan seems to be over the worst of his discomfort and slowly growing his sea legs. He has begun venturing from his bed, and we have at last had the opportunity to make a prolonged conversation. Having a cabin-mate with whom I can converse offers a great relief for me. He has even indicated that he would be interested in playing cards to pass our evenings. I have found myself longing for the jovial company of Arthur Cartwright. While Doungan seems pleasant enough, he is a naturally quiet man and lacks the same boisterous familiarity that I grew so fond of in Arthur.

Monday, 20th May 1816

The weather continues much the same, and the monotony of my days begin to grow. I am also feeling more unsure of myself. The ship cuts cleanly through the waves, but I seem to sense its every movement. I cannot recall feeling so unsettled on my inward journey. My stomach has not felt easy since the storm. While I am able to eat and hold my food, I cannot seem to settle the bile that has risen in my belly.

Possibly due to this increased sensitivity, I have also found a heightening of my seasickness when I read or write, a malady I have not suffered before. I can manage a few minutes, but then my stomach churns and I am forced to put it aside. I had hoped that I might distract myself further with this journal, but it seems my constitution would dictate otherwise.

Monday, 16th September 1816

It has been some months since I last opened this journal. I had not originally intended for it to become a personal diary, and on my homeward voyage this intention was joined by the acute sickness I developed whenever I attempted to read or write aboard ship. And, of course, since my arrival back on England's shores my health has prescripted me from any such work.

But now, as my convalescence comes to an end, I find myself seeking distraction. My aunt will not even hear of my returning to London, yet now my body is mostly recovered I crave something to occupy my thoughts. To that end I have sought this journal out once more. Part of the recovery of any great trauma, I firmly believe, is examining that which you have endured. Sitting here now in the pleasant Hampshire sunshine with the comforting smells of the farm filling the air around me, I shall recount my ordeal in the hope that it shall no longer weigh upon my thoughts.

Upon leaving Buenos Aires and weathering that first storm, we continued on in fair condition for the majority of the voyage. While the weather was never as fine or as even as it was those first few days, we did not encounter any truly rough weather until the very end. I found myself handling the trip far less well than I had my outward journey. Perhaps it was some lingering effect of my fever, some weakening of my constitution, but now it took far less motion to unsettle my ear and stomach. I soon found I could not even think of reading whilst we were in motion, and even standing for too long would set my legs shaking.

While I did not think my illness anything remarkable, it

must have shown more on my face than I believed. I often felt the gaze of both sailor and passenger as I passed through the ship's walkways. The looks did not linger, and I did not catch them staring openly, but I felt their regard and I took it as indication that I had to do what I must to protect my wellbeing. Despite my unsettled stomach I ate all I could, and rested whenever I felt weak. I did not wish to exert myself and overwork my weakened constitution.

It did not help that the motions of the ship at night soon led me to suffer uncomfortable dreams. I would wake sweating, with vague memories of images and visions that fled from my conscious mind. They did not tax me overmuch, but they did leave me each morning with a lingering sense of unease.

From this point in my narrative I must admit to a vagueness of memory. While I am certain I was no more than casually unwell throughout the whole of the journey, I can no longer recall much of it. Since that final storm, the monotonous days that led up to it have blended together in my mind. I can recall snippets of our stops on the African coast, hazy images of unfamiliar ports and exotic peoples, but little else.

Strangely enough, my clearest memories of this time are my dreams. Wavering and elusive as they were, they are yet my only certain memories; nightmares where our ship fell apart around me, or where I was trapped within some cell or box. I cannot recall precise details of individual nights, just the recurring themes and fears that returned night after night. As much as it defies explanation, their existence and frequency is more certain to me than any other aspect of my voyage.

The cause of this amnesia struck us on the final leg of our journey. It is an event I find it hard to recount, even now.

Having made our way from Africa and around the Spanish

coast without incident, we at last left the Atlantic and were on the cusp of the English Channel. I can recall feeling excitement, that after so long I was finally to see my homeland again.

That night the *April Mercy* was struck by the fiercest storm I believe any man could possibly imagine. The day had been calm, but in a matter of minutes our vessel was surrounded by a furious vortex of thick dark clouds that blew in and filled the previously empty sky. If I had not been on deck at the time and witnessed it with my own eyes I would not have believed any climate could alter so quickly. It was as if nature itself had decided to focus all its anger and hurl its full might against us. We passengers fled below decks while the brave crew desperately battled to defend their ship against the sudden tempest.

The storm racked and tossed the ship back and forth across the Channel with wild abandon, tearing sails and flinging shattering timbers into the churning ocean. Several crewmen were washed overboard. For a week at least we were thrown back and forth across the Channel. My sickness returned with full force, and even had I wished to I could not have summoned the strength to leave my bunk. I could not eat. Each night I dreamt of the ship falling apart around me, only to wake to find myself still huddled in my blankets mumbling fevered prayers. Often I would feel Doungan's eyes on me as I lay there moaning, but had no strength to turn to him. I can half recall overheard conversations outside our door, the crew and officers expressing their fears for our survival, but I cannot be sure if they were real or just some fragment of my nightmares.

When finally the winds died down enough for the ship to limp into Portsmouth harbour, the *April Mercy* was as close to a wreck as could still be afloat. It looked as if it had undergone a battle rather than a simple voyage. The wind still blew, even here in the harbour, and tattered sail and lengths of rope flapped in the air, snapping back against wet canvas and wood. More than one crewman sat with blooded bandages around useless limbs, while those who had escaped injury guided us in.

I wish I could have felt more for those brave souls who had battled to bring us home, but at this point I was no more than a pitiable wreck of a man. The voyage from Buenos Aires had stripped me of what strength I had regained after my illness, and that final great storm had almost been too much to endure. I was now nothing but a thing of bone and rag, my memories in tatters. I cannot recall how long I had gone without a meal. The idea of my eating had been unthinkable for the duration of the storm. Gaunt and loose, I required carrying from my cabin. Once ashore I found I could not even stand, my legs tipping me aside whenever I made the attempt. I recall feeling the eyes of onlookers regarding us as we arrived. What sorry wretches we must have appeared.

I was taken to a nearby doctor, who did what he could for the worst of the sickness and allowed me to rest. Here is my first clear memory; lying in the cold, bare room as my carer built up the fire and forced restoratives down my throat. Knowing that in my current state the next leg of my journey home to London was beyond me, I was able to give the address of an aunt living near the town of Romsey, not too far from Portsmouth. Thanking God for such serendipity, I dictated a letter and paid for it to be delivered. Doing so seemed to sap what little strength I had left to me, for having done so I fell at once back into oblivion.

I sank into a delirium, and have no notion of what time passed before my cousin David arrived with his family's horse and trap. All I can recall are more dreams and illusions floating before my eyes; the half wrought nightmares that had followed me from abroad. I am told I lapsed once again into the fever. Clearly it had remained in my blood all this time, to burst out when my strength reached its lowest ebb. It had me firm in its grasp when David arrived, and I remember nothing of the trip to the farm or of anything before waking in my aunt's guest room with the English summer sun streaming through the window onto my face. I felt weaker than I had ever done in my life, even more so than when I had first contracted this illness, but for the first time in weeks I felt safe.

For the whole of the last fortnight I have rested under the expert care of my dear aunt. The eldest sister of my mother, she and her husband own this good sized farm here in Hampshire. I spent a number of summers visiting this place during my childhood, and the familiarity of those memories does my spirit good. My cousins, all my own age, and their families make an extended workforce, working the land and caring for the dairy cows that make their trade. Since my arrival they have, to a man, tended me without rest or complaint. My days are spent sitting in the yard with the comforting smells of the animals all around me, their shabby old tomcat, which I can recall playing with as a kitten, curled in my lap.

Oh, to be in England. Never have I appreciated my own country more. With each breath I feel my soul renew. Once strong enough, by my aunt's stringent judgement, I composed a number of letters; one to my mother to follow up my aunt's epistle on my condition, and another to the firm to appraise them of my whereabouts and wellbeing. By this time they would have been long expecting my return. I had been in no condition to pass on a London bound message when I left Portsmouth, and this was the first opportunity to do so.

My body has now regained much of its strength and the dreams have retreated from my mind. My nights remain tinged with a feeling of disquiet I cannot seem to shake, but time will heal all. Now I begin to grow restless for stimulation. While I cannot say I am keen to leave the paradise of this English farmstead at such a glorious time of year, I know I cannot sit so inactive for much longer. My trunk sits in my room, unopened since my return other than to ensure all my papers were undamaged. I know soon I shall hear from my employers, and will have to begin my return to London. But for now, at least, I can rest.

Wednesday, 19th September 1816

Today I received a return letter from Mr. Dennings himself. It seems my idyllic rest must soon come to an end. They had been expecting my return some time ago, and had begun to fear the worst as reports of the weather across the Atlantic came in. He acknowledged my illness and need for recovery, but has dictated its end. Earl Sebastian is apparently champing at the bit to be done with this business, and has instructed I be brought to the Leer estates at the earliest opportunity to report in person. Mr. Dennings will travel here, and then together we shall carry onwards to Wiltshire.

It is understandable if a certain moroseness overcomes me. I have greatly enjoyed my time here with my family. It has been a happy two weeks, even if I have been unwell. I shall be sorry to leave them. My aunt is unhappy with my recall coming so soon, and I have had to make it plain that the Earl is not the sort of man to be kept waiting, and also the importance this encounter has for my future career. In truth I would rather remain for a good while longer, but that is not my charge.

I worry when I recall my state of mind last time I dedicated myself to my research. After the effect it had on me, I find I am not keen to return to it. However I must face my worries, and ensure my work is in order for Mr. Dennings' arrival. A Sandings shall not be found wanting in his duty. Hopefully the encapsulation of this business will be a simple task and the Earl will not wish more than a cursory explanation. Then this whole damn thing can be forgotten.

Friday, 27th September 1816

I am tired. Both travel and the experience of an interrogation by Earl Sebastian have sapped what strength I had. While I am not nearly as bad as I was when I returned to this country a month ago, if my aunt could see the state to which I have been reduced I wager she would have a few words to say even to the Earl.

Mr. Dennings arrived at the farm late on Wednesday evening. A tall, sober man, Mr. Dennings has always put me in mind of a schoolmaster expecting me to make some slip in my Latin. But while he lacks the open nature of Mr. Caine, he is not an unpleasant man. He was most gracious to my family, commenting on my recovery and the quality of my aunt's nursing. The sight of my employer, ever the quintessential city gentleman, sitting to dinner with my rural farming cousins was a strange one. I have never dined with either of my employers before, and cannot say the scene was as I would have envisioned it.

We left together the following morning. My cousin David took us to where we could take a coach to Salisbury and then on to Parrel House; the ancestral seat of the Leer family. I had never visited the place before, of course, so was keen for my first look at this famous home. As we made our way up the long driveway the impressive building rose up ahead. It dominated the lands around, yet I could not help but recognise the signs of relative poverty that marred it. The pathway was pitted and in poor condition, and the lawns more ragged than I would have expected from such a distinguished home. Once we pulled in I could also see that much of the masonry of the frontage needed work; there were many cracks and places where decoration had fallen. While Parrel House remains more than impressive, the effects of Edgar's mismanagement and disinterest can be plainly seen.

We were greeted at the door by Earl Sebastian and his wife. They had been married just before I had left for South America. He was as I recalled him from our one previous meeting in London; a tall, stern man with dark hair and piercing eyes whose presence dominated those around him. Since the last time I had seen him he had grown a beard, and the addition only added to the authority of his appearance. The new Lady Leer, whom I had not met before, was a slim little thing, though her gaze showed a firm strength of character. I cannot imagine the Earl would have the temperament to tolerate a weak minded wife. I was given to understand Earl Sebastian had refused to consider marriage until he had come into the dignity, and so had wed relatively late in life. While I had been away they had been blesses with the birth of a son, one Edward Arthur. So now while the financial prospects of the family were still questionable, the bloodline at least was secure.

We were shown to our rooms and informed that the Earl would speak to us in his study before dinner. It seemed, as ever, he wished to settle the business as soon as could be. I myself had no desire to drag things out and so readily prepared my notes. I was given time to wash and change, then a footman came to lead me to the study. Folders in hand, I made my way along the portrait-lined corridors to my destination.

What hopes I had held that the interview would be concise

and to the point were rapidly dashed. It seems that despite the Earl's wish to be done with the business, he would in no way condone it to be rushed. Indeed, he wanted a meticulous degree of detail. Sitting at his desk, with myself and Mr. Dennings seated opposite, he at once and without preamble instructed me to begin a discourse of my time in Buenos Aires. I told him of my arrival and interviews with the city's officials. At the appropriate points I produced my copies of all the documents pertaining to his father's arrival, marriage, and death within the city. Earl Sebastian took each and gave them a cursory glance to witness their contents before putting them to one side for Mr. Dennings to collect.

The marriage forms and certificates of the birth of young Tobias brought a sneer from his otherwise sober expression. These were thrown aside with palpable distaste, with instructions to Mr. Dennings that they be dealt with in the correct manner. I assume this relates to the Earl's efforts to ensure the legal disownment of the mother and child, but they were not mentioned here.

I had hoped from this point the interview would be concluded, but once the legalities were done the Earl Sebastian took me in his gaze and instructed me to recount for him the full tale of his father's time in the city; what he had been about, who he had fraternised with, and what activities he had undertaken. I quailed under his gaze, for he spoke in a manner which made me feel as if I was somehow culpable via association. I had not been expecting to have to give so much detail. Mr. Dennings spoke and told me it was required as the Earl wished to know as much as about his father's actions and dealings as possible, to pre-empt any unexpected consequences to the family that might somehow arise in the future. By knowing everything, the Earl could prepare for any eventualities.

Girding myself, for I had wholeheartedly wished to avoid

recounting these tales once again, I told the story of Earl Edgar's time in Buenos Aires as I had learned it; from his arrival to the city without his wife, his marriage to Maria Juanita, and his actions and personality within the city. As I spoke I felt a great unease, for I had no knowledge of how the son might react to hearing such things about the father. The Earl simply sat and listened, his gaze pinning me to the chair. My face reddened as I recounted the lewd accounts of Edgar's household, but nothing seemed to shake Earl Sebastian. He simply sat and listened, asking the occasional question on some matter or other, or verifying the validity of my source. He gave the impression of a man who had long ago accepted the lifestyle of his father, and had determined never to be shocked or embarrassed by it again.

On reaching the account of Edgar's final days, Earl Sebastian's first question was to enquire about the documents that had been found with his body. I gave a silent prayer of thanks that Arthur Cartwright had been given the foresight to ask on them, for I perceived the notion that not having procured them would have been a gross misstep. Picking through my folders, I located the bound sheaf of burnt and crumpled papers. Upon unbinding them and touching the sheets, I was overcome by a sudden wave of nausea. My heart began to race and my skin felt clammy and cold. For that moment my memories were dragged back to those terrible days of sickness in Señor Mercallo's rooms. I was struck by an irrefutable certainty that there was another in the room with us, standing over my shoulder. I turned, but there was no one there. The room contained no one other than myself, the Earl, and Mr. Dennings.

This must have struck me visibly, for Mr. Dennings pointedly cleared his throat, calling me back to the matter at hand. I begged pardon for the lapse, blaming a momentary weakness remaining from my illness. The Earl irritably signalled for me to continue, and I quickly passed the papers over. He began to idly shuffle through them, giving each a cursory glance before letting it drop to the table and moving on to the next. My eyes were drawn to every one. Somehow my previous fascination had been reawakened, and I was overwhelmed by the urge, the need, to solve this puzzle I was only half sure existed.

Eventually the sheets had all been regarded and sat in an untidy pile on the Earl's desk. He asked me if I had examined them and, when I replied in the affirmative, asked if I had discovered anything that seemed legally relevant. I replied in the negative, but noted the one sheet that seemed to refer to the Lady Margaret, his mother. He handed them over and I carefully located the one I had mentioned. Thankfully the nausea did not strike again as I gripped the pages. He read it for a moment, then tossed it away. I was shocked at the man's lack of regard for his parents or remorse for their passing, but remembered who those parents had been and what they had done. Earl Sebastian had been abandoned here as a baby, and had maybe seen his uncaring parents half a dozen times in his whole life. He had grown up watching as his father summoned and spent his family fortune on a scandalous and immoral lifestyle across the breadth of the world. I know for a certainty that Sebastian had at various times attempted to wrestle legal control of the estate away from his absentee father, but each attempt had been rebuffed and so his career in Whitehall was all that remained him to keep the house going. I later learned his wife, the Lady Sofia, was the younger daughter of an eminent politician. The marriage had brought the Leer family an amount of political capital, but its financial status is still, at this point, far from certain.

Satisfied that all was in order, Earl Sebastian tossed the papers to Mr. Dennings. As far as he was concerned, as long as the firm was confident that they contained nothing of legal import, then they were of no further use and were to be disposed of. I knew neither Mr. Dennings or Mr. Caine would let the sheets, the last words of one of the Earls Leer, be destroyed. They would be filed and lodged in the family records back in London. But as far as the present Earl was concerned, they were of no significance.

Finally satisfied I had recounted all I could, Earl Sebastian then spoke with Mr. Dennings while I sat and caught my breath. My job done, it seemed I was of little interest to the Earl, and they discussed the finalising of certain legal procedures that had required my return as though I were not present. Mr. Dennings assured the Earl that with my notes, the firm would be able to complete the business in as short a time as possible and he could foresee no problems arising. I was not referred to by name, but was under the distinct impression that I would be heavily involved with the work, a prospect which greatly buoys my flagging spirits. While I would be more than grateful to not have to concentrate on this business any longer, to be assigned to it permanently would mean a great step up in my career.

The interview complete, we were dismissed to change for dinner. The experience of dining at Parrel House is one that shall stay with me for the rest of my life. Never have I sat with such an august company, even one lowered to such straits as the Leers. The food was simple enough, and nothing was served that I have not eaten before in lesser situations, but never to such quality. We began with a soup almost clear in consistency, yet filled with such a burst of fresh flavour as danced on the tongue. The beef we were then served was rich and tender, seeping with juices and served with vegetables fresh from the summer harvest. And the wine! Never before had I tasted such fine vintage. I am glad my unease in such a setting prevented any thoughts of indulgence, for the wines served were sharp and crisp and held a smoothness far removed from any I have drunk before. Even still, when I stood at the end of the evening I must admit to a lightheadedness unrelated to my passing sickness.

The meal was marred, unfortunately, by the sense of a hovering presence that had remained since the meeting in the study. At no point could I shake the feeling that someone stood uncomfortably close behind me. I felt greatly agitated, and each time the footmen leant over or passed by me I would twitch uncontrollably. I had hoped to make a good impression with the family and Mr. Dennings, but I fear my constitution prevented this opportunity. All evening I remained so afflicted, until I retired to my room and fell into a blessedly rapid and dreamless sleep.

This morning I awoke refreshed, if a little groggy. I found my unease from the previous evening had passed and so happily attributed it to a nervousness caused by my surroundings, so much grander than those I am used to, and my interrogation by the Earl. After a long sickness and then weeks on a quiet country farm, who would not feel shaken at such an evening?

Mr. Dennings and I are due to take a coach back to London tomorrow morning so as to be back for the start of the week, which gave us today to enjoy our surroundings. I found myself breakfasting alone, which was agreeable after my discomfort in dining with the family. After I had eaten, I took myself out for a walk around the grounds.

Parrel House dates back hundreds of years, though of course none of that original structure remains. The current building dates back to the sixteen hundreds, and is notably lacking in a number of modernisations and improvements most homes of the sort would have had done over the last fifty years. In the lifetimes of the previous two Earls, one so short and the other lived in total disregard for the building, Parrel House has been forced to go without. The place sits with an archaic and worn air, but nevertheless holds an unmistakable grandeur.

Unfortunately, my good mood did not last the morning. While walking I encountered the young child, Edward, being taken for a turn around the grounds by his nurse. I made my introduction and took a look at the future Earl. The child was a healthy looking boy, with a strength to him that reminded me of his father. Looking at him laying in his carriage, I found myself wondering how his blood would tell. Would he take after his father, or would he be wild and dangerous like his grandfather Edgar? However, the thought was brief, for it was the nurse who took my attention and thus turned my mood.

The nurse was younger than I expected, but then I often find those holding such roles strangely young. It is odd to think that positions which once had such authority over me are now so often held by those of my own age. She was attractive, with firm plump cheeks and inviting eyes that regarded me with clear appraisal. She was dressed modestly, as was proper, but a few strands of dark hair hung down from her cap in a most alluring fashion. We talked a while, and she seemed to show a genuine interest in me.

As the young child slept, we spoke of my journeys abroad. I admit I was enjoying the attention and a little thrown, but certainly not put off, by her forward manner. When I mentioned that I would be leaving in the morning she stepped close to me and whispered that if I wished it, she would be able to meet me that night at a point near the servants quarters where she could find us a place no one would disturb us.

Immediately I felt as if someone had stepped out behind us. I spun around, fearing either my or her employer had come up unseen. There was no one there. Nobody was even close by. I imagine having the clear space around to see should anyone approach us was the reason she felt safe to be so brazen. She giggled, clearly thinking my movement simply caused by a fear we might be overheard, and assured me again we would be more than safe from discovery. But it was not that which made me feel such a sudden distemper in my stomach. A year or so ago I may well have happily jumped at the chance she offered, but as soon as the image of what her dark eyes were promising filled my mind I was struck with a nauseous bile. All the disquieting feelings that had filled me when I learned the tales of Edgar and Maria returned. While I had no intention of sinking to such levels as they had, I could not drag my mind away from the memories of their actions; such lewd and uncivil images that do not bear repeating. Flushed and uneasy, I made hasty excuses and fled the nanny's presence.

The sensation has remained with me all day, and I fear for what it may mean. Can it simply be an artefact of my illness? On leaving the nurse and child I found myself in the library, mercifully alone, and spent the remainder of the day hidden away in an attempt to distract myself. But whatever books I found, my mind continued to reel with unwelcome images; the wanton and repulsive scenes that had been described to me, amplified and magnified by my own imagination to a point where they seemed they might burst forth from my mind. I could do nothing to find relief, and by suppertime was a shaking, quivering wreck.

I begged off attending dinner, claiming my weakness had struck again. Mr. Dennings commented on my pallor and general complexion when I met him in the hallway, and agreed I should take an early rest. Rather than join the family for dinner I took a tray in my room, which sits cooling beside me now as I attempt to rest my mind that I might sleep. I pray that perhaps writing down these event might aid in structuring my thoughts, an aid for concentration I have found to be effective in the past. While it seems to have managed to calm the angry, prurient visions, it has left my mind focused on the troubles my time in Romsey had allowed me to forget.

And still I am bothered by this persistent sense that some unseen person regards me somehow. Even now, as I sit here at the writing desk in my room, I am compelled to look into the corner over and over again, convinced some eye regards me. Twice this evening, while writing this entry, I have had to give in to my paranoia and check for gaps or spy-holes in the wall, minutely searching the curtains to ensure they adequately cover the windowpane. A ridiculous notion, as my room is on the second floor and the only way anyone might see in clearly would be to climb the wall below.

Hopefully sleep will rid me of this distemper. I wish to make a good impression on Mr. Dennings on our journey tomorrow, and in my current state I fear I shall make no decent travel companion.

Sunday, 29th September 1816

London. At last I am truly home. On arriving in the city I took my leave from Mr. Dennings and returned to my old lodgings. The firm had ensured that my rent was paid and all necessary attentions were maintained so that they would remain ready for me when I returned. It is a strange feeling. Having been away for so long, they are at once both familiar to me and strange. I cannot say whether it is some quirk of the mind, or if my perceptions have changed after my voyages, but the room seems so much smaller than I remember it.

I did not sleep well that final night at Parrel House, but awoke feeling far more myself than I had been and was able to put the uncomfortable encounter with the comely nanny behind me. I still felt a little weak, the stresses of travelling lingering within me. Steeling myself for the unavoidable final stretch to London, I set upon a full and hearty breakfast to fortify me for the journey. As before, I arrived at the breakfast room to find it empty save for myself, but as I ate I was joined by Mr. Dennings. He commented on my improved appearance and agreed on my conclusions regarding my illness. He promised me a couple of days to rest after we returned to the city before he would expect my return to work. I did not wish to have to accept such charity, fearing it did not reflect well on my prospects for promotion, but could find little reason to refuse.

The day was pleasant, and we made good time. As we travelled, Mr. Dennings and I discussed the legal points raised in our meeting with the Earl. From all indications, I am convinced I am indeed to be entrusted with the charge of finishing the business, which means good things for my position with the firm. Discussing the cold facts and clear practices, avoiding all the unpleasant elements the Earl had insisted upon my recounting, helped clear my head and I felt in great spirits.

After a while the two of us exhausted what business could be discussed on this ride, and we lapsed into intermittent small talk. I was still in awe of Mr. Dennings, being my employer and a man of some standing in London, yet by all indications he seemed pleased with my work. He implied that Earl Sebastian had expressed his satisfaction with the outcome of my trip, and with my handling of the affair. He then asked a few polite questions, mercifully avoiding mentioning Earl Edgar and allowing me to recall my happier experiences abroad.

But after a while, quite in passing, Mr. Dennings made a comment that has stuck in my mind. It seems a little thing, but I find myself quite unable to dismiss it. While discussing the unpleasantness of my return voyage, he told me how the final storm that had struck the *April Mercy* off the south coast, just outside of Portsmouth, was, according to available records, remarkably similar to the one that had sunk the *Endeavour*, taking the lives of Earl Andrew and his wife and leaving the young Edgar parentless.

On hearing this, a weight settled into my stomach and a wave of nausea crashed over me. I was certain, though I do not know how, that these two storms, so many years apart, were one and the same. Clearly this discomfort showed upon my face, for Mr. Dennings commented on my complexion and profusely apologised for bringing up what must have been an unpleasant memory.

We spoke little for the rest of the journey. I curse the weakness that curtailed this opportunity to ingratiate myself with Mr. Dennings, but as much as I might try I could not shake this feeling. While it has faded slightly, overtaken by the business of getting about the city and finding my way home, when I awoke this morning I was still unable to forget this apparently coincidental fact. still thinking on it. What am I to make of this? Can it simply be coincidence? I try to convince myself, but cannot shake the feeling that it has to be some deeper meaning behind it.

Wednesday, 2ⁿᵈ October 1816

Today I returned to work to be straight away called into Mr Caine and Mr. Dennings' office. I shall admit that I felt nervous as I stepped through into that impressive room. I need not have. My ambitions have been met and my efforts vindicated. They are pleased with my actions and behaviours abroad, and I am being advanced within the company!

All my work, all my efforts have paid off. The whole reason I was willing to travel such distance was towards this goal. No one in my family has ever risen so high as I. I am to take on responsibility for all work regarding the Leer family within the firm, which is no small honour. While I hope that this Argentinian business might be quickly resolved, I will gladly endure what I must now that it comes accompanied by this greater rank.

With these responsibilities comes a notable rise in my salary, and I plan to look around for finer accommodation. Then I must write to my mother and inform her of this news. The expense they put into my education is now paid off. While I may have railed against it at the time, I now cannot say how grateful I am to my parents for expending the cost and enduring my apathy.

In my euphoria I even cared little for the looks I felt as I exited the office. I did not catch any of the other clerks peering over, but I cannot expect my elevation would not raise at least a little envy. The rest of the morning I spent arranging my new desk. I have been given a place almost next to the office of my employers, a fine signifier of my promotion. I began my new work with a feeling of elation. I cannot think I was possibly concentrating as fully as I should, and shall be forced to review my work tomorrow. But I cannot berate myself. Today my spirits are as high as ever they have been.

Friday, 4th October 1816

My life is busier than it has been in a long time. Since returning to work and taking on my new responsibilities I find my work hours and the effort required far exceeds that which I was used to even before my convalescence. I have left late each evening with little energy for much more than a late meal and to crawl into bed.

While I had been travelling, my previous duties had been given over to Andrew Palin, another of the firm's clerks. He now works under me as I finalise Earl Edgar's business. Together we have spent the last couple of days drawing up the necessary documents and ensuring all the final details of the probate were clear and legal. There have been no attempts to block any of the proceedings while I was away, and so there is little impediment to our task. Soon I shall be able to put the trip firmly behind me.

And yet, I have been unable to forget what Mr. Dennings told me. I cannot shake that last coincidence of the *Endurance* and the *April Mercy*. How can it be that the two ships could be struck by such storms at the same point? And when I think upon it, how natural could anyone consider that storm? As much as I wish I could not, I can so clearly recall how the dark clouds filled a clear sky so fast and so unnaturally. While much of that voyage still lies within a murky forgetfulness, that moment I see with such stark clarity. What was it that struck our ship? None who had been at its centre could call what we faced a natural summer storm.

Thursday, 10th October 1816

I have discovered more. I don't know whether this was fortune or folly, but I had the chance to delve deeper into this mystery that beset me and I took it. Now my mind is even more mired in questions and fears. I sought to find answers, but what I have learned has only taken me further along this path of uncertainty and question.

Palin and I had completed all our work, and the business of Earl Edgar's probate was finally resolved. All the required paperwork had been created and filed, and I knew that at last I could put my malefic trip behind me. With what I know of Earl Sebastian's plans and ambitions I am all but certain that I shall never have to consider his sinful father ever again. All I had remaining was to archive our reports and the papers I had brought from Argentina, including Earl Edgar's ravings.

These had been neatly bound in a leather cover for storage. Both Mr. Dennings and Mr. Caine had poured over them to ensure they contained no lost points of legal interest, but seemed happy with my initial judgement that there was nothing that should concern us. Neither of them had been struck by those haunting words as I had. While all that anyone else sees are the nonsense writings of a madman, to me they remain an elusive riddle that lurks in the back of my mind.

The firm's long term archives are kept in the basement of the building. Walls of covered shelves store forms and reports dating back decades. As I was putting all the new documents in their place in the section devoted to the Leer family, it suddenly occurred to me there would be extensive reports on the death of Earl Andrew here. Mr. Dennings' story of the *Endeavour* came back to me, and I realised that if the storm that struck that ship had indeed been the same as the one that hit my own then I could likely find evidence here. Perhaps, I thought, the old man's memory had simply made up the connection. Here would be proof. If I wished to know for sure the facts of the sinking I had only to search for them. Morbid curiosity overtook me and, to my own foolishness, I began to search back along the shelves.

It took me only a few moments to locate the answers I sought. Tucked away in a dusty folder I found a collection of papers all pertaining to the death of Earl Andrew, collected and bound by the firm at the time. Alongside other pertinent documents was a copy of the Admiralty report regarding the

Endeavour and its final voyage. I took it aside to the nearby reading desk.

Endeavour had been a fairly modern ship for its time. It had been sailing up from the Mediterranean Sea, where it had been carrying cargos from the African continent. For some reason not documented, for it would seem to me to have been far out of its way, the ship sailed by way of Ireland and docked in Cork before beginning the final leg of its journey to London. It was here Earl Andrew and the Lady Annabel boarded the ship. They had been travelling back from overseeing the family's Irish estates and joined the vessel for the fateful final leg of its voyage, where it was struck by the storm and sunk with the loss of all hands.

Reading the report, a shiver went down my spine. Hard storms had been reported across the entire channel in the days preceding the sinking, but nothing of such ferocity as that final tempest. The report stated that the storm came in unusually quickly, and that the sinking happened within sight of Portsmouth harbour.

I shuddered at reading these words, and the basement seemed almost to grow darker around me. Could it have been just a coincidence? I pray so. Earl Edgar's words, written in his final, maddened days, floated back into my mind. He wrote of his father's death, and of something within the *Endeavour*. What had Edgar known?

Despite knowing it was folly to continue, I recovered Edgar's papers, now in their leather cover, and laid them upon the desk. All the time my soul beseeched me not to continue in this foolish path, to leave these dark murmured thoughts to the past and retreat from that place. Yet an unshakeable fascination pulled me on. Such a mood as draws crowds to Newgate on execution day; we know good men should not feel so, but macabre fascination pulls at our baser instincts and overwhelms rational sense.

Letting the pages fall open, the familiar handwriting stared up at me from the tattered and burned sheets as I sought out the relevant passage.

So little did father know. Oh Andrew, Earl Andrew and foolish mother. All alone and son far away. No idea could he have had what all at once lay within Endeavour. So evil, so dark.

That one phrase had lain upon my memory, drawing me back; "lay within Endeavour." What did he speak of? Surely not more coincidence and happenstance? Once more I went to the old file, searching for more information that might disprove my fears. Within I found a shipping manifest; a list of passengers, the Earl and his wife's names amongst them, and a long list of cargo. Amongst the more mundane items, the ship had been carrying crates from Egypt bound for the British Museum.

My blood ran cold. Egypt? That other mention made by Edgar; Ptalantohtep. When first I read it I had thought the name had an Egyptian feel. Could this be linked? Perhaps in other circumstances I might have managed to think otherwise, but in that dark basement, lit only by the glow of my oil lamp, the connection hung over me like a shroud.

This was enough, at last, to throw me from this foolish curiosity. A mortal fear gripped my heart and I once again felt that same strange presence behind me. I spun around, but saw no one. Grabbing the lantern I turned and cast it around the study, but its light fell on nothing but insubstantial shadow. In a sudden desperation I gathered the papers from the desk. In my haste I tripped, sending the sheets to fall haphazardly across the floor. Dropping to my knees, I pulled them back into a rough pile. Panic had taken hold of me and I could make no sense of the order I should have striven for. My mind was filled with the need to get out of that dark, enclosing room as soon as possible.

It was at that moment that my eyes were caught by a report that by chance had worked its way to the top of the untidy pile. It appeared to be a cutting from a news-sheet, dusty and yellowing, that made mention of the *Endeavour*. Perhaps it was that word that caught my eye. Whatever the reason, I stopped my hurried shuffling and began to read.

The report spoke of a remarkable discovery made in Egypt regarding the cargo believed to be carried by the *Endeavour*. The ship was engaged to transport a number of artefacts from an excavation in Egypt, led by a Professor Windome. It seems he had uncovered some ancient tomb, and the relics he had recovered therein were bound for London to be displayed at the British Museum. Obviously, when *Endeavour* sank, all those concerned were devastated at the loss of such important and valuable archaeological finds. Yet barely days after the sinking, news arrived from Egypt that the cargo that had supposedly been aboard the doomed vessel had been discovered, unharmed, in a warehouse in Cairo. Through some twist of happenstance it had never been loaded onto the ship.

I shook as I read this. My panic had subsided by now, replaced by an eerie disquiet. This only added to the list of the uncanny associations to my voyage. I had noted, when first I read Edgar's notes, how certain words had smacked of the Egyptian. Could this have been what had intrigued Edgar? He mentioned things that "lay within Endeavour". Such a mystery could indeed have interested such a mind as his.

At last common sense overtook me. I hastily thrust the papers back on the shelves before fleeing the cloying basement to cleaner air above.

Yet although I fled the building, I can not escape the knowledge I had uncovered. Oh how I wish I had possessed the strength to ignore the perverse urge to seek out more! I could almost consider myself bewitched that I had continued in this folly.

I know it is a childish whim, and far below one of my station, but I cannot shake the idea that the two storms are connected. That there is some link between the force that sank the *Endeavour* and that which so desperately tried to do the same to the *April Mercy*. Recalling the condition of the *April Mercy* as it had finally limped into the harbour, I thank God it was a more modern and robust vessel and thus able to face the tempest and come through where the *Endeavour* had floundered.

I have since found it impossible to relax. My investigations have set me on edge. I will leave my lamp burning tonight. I chide myself for a fool, but I cannot face again the darkness that has haunted my mind since I fled the archives.

Saturday, 12th October 1816

I have at last had the opportunity to seek out new accommodation. With my increased salary I had decided upon better lodgings nearer to the office. My recent long hours have highlighted the distance I travel each day, and living closer will allow me greater freedom with my time.

I have found rooms overlooking a fine street in Holborn, and on taking a walk this morning I found myself near the British Museum. I had visited there before, though with little purpose other than idle education. With my afternoon free, I decide the day would be well spent bettering myself and made my way towards its magnificent edifice.

At least, I told myself it was merely a whim, but before long I found myself in the Egyptian rooms. I do not know what delusion led me to that place. Perhaps it was simply coincidence, and idle wandering simply brought me there by chance. Whatever the reason, once I was there a morbid curiosity overtook my mind. All yesterday I had felt foolish for the childish fears I had felt in the archives. A man of my station should show a sterner mettle than I had done that night, and so I determined to face this mystery head on. My mind, I told myself, was simply overcome with suspicion and superstition, and so I determined I would smother such base, animal fears with cold, established facts.

I sought out one of the staff and enquired about anyone who might know details of the voyage of the *Endeavour*, or the work of Professor Windome. So many years after the event I held little hope anyone present would recall it. However, I was introduced to a gentleman about twenty years my elder, one Dr. David Soll. He was one of the curators of the museum and, as it turned out, a student of Windome's work. Being such an unusual event, the business of the *Endeavour* was one that had always stuck in his mind, and he was happy to recount it and answer whatever questions he could.

The thin, scholarly man took me aside to a small office, away from the curiosities and displays. Settling in, he asked me what I wished to know. Unwilling to make mention of my more foolish worries, I merely told him my position and that the name had come up during an investigation into the history of the Leer family. I passed it off as a simple fancy; a peak of interest after reading of the work of Professor Windome and the artefacts that had supposedly been bound for London.

Dr Soll leant back in his chair and took on an air of one used to teaching such histories. Professor Windome, he told me, was a scholar and explorer who had been travelling Egypt, searching for the treasures that history and rumour promised lay waiting for those lucky or skilled enough to discover them. Around this time, reports of a lost temple uncovered by a rogue sandstorm had reached him. He had hurried to the location and rapidly established a camp in order to fully excavate it before the desert could once again reclaim it. Apparently the site was a marvel, with an astounding number of artefacts and items amazingly well preserved by the desert sands. Once the excavation was established, Windome engaged a shipping company to aid him in delivering some of his finds to the then newly opened British Museum, in order to gain public interest and greater funding for his efforts. The artefacts were transported to Cairo, and from there onto the *Endeavour*.

When the news of the sinking reached Egypt, Windome had been sent into an incalculable fury. Some of the greatest finds in archaeological history, not to mention months of work, lost to the ocean floor on the very last leg of the voyage. It was then, Dr. Soll told me with an undisguised relish for the mystery, that all the artefacts thought lost were discovered in the warehouse in the city. The company employed to load the finds onto the ship had been doing an inventory of their stock and found the crates, safe and undisturbed. Windome refused to allow them to be shipped over sea again and they remained in Egypt until after his death.

This event caused no small amount of uproar, as all involved were certain that *some* cargo had been loaded aboard the ship and been lost in its place. I pressed Dr. Soll for more details. There had been an investigation, of course, but no missing cargo was ever identified and no one ever came forward to claim on the loss. Here he leant in conspiratorially to tell me how many believed some kind of smuggling had been involved. He could give me no hard facts.

I had hoped for something more concrete, some earthly

information about this strange recovery. Something that had come to light since the initial report. So far his words had simply verified those facts I had learned from that dusty report in the basement. I wanted more knowledge, something that would dispel the air of the supernatural rather than substantiate it. With nothing to reassure me I felt my apprehensions returning. I had just one more question, and how I wish I had not stayed to ask it. Steeling myself for the answer, I enquired whether the temple Professor Windome had been investigating had any particular name or patron.

Dr. Soll sat back. It is not an easy thing, he informed me, identifying Egyptian ruins. The hieroglyphics those ancient people used are all but incomprehensible. Those who study such things are forced to resort to documents written in Greek and Latin. He told me there were several known to refer to the area and using those, along with local rumour and legend, Windome had collated a list of probable names. There had been several thrown around by scholars over the years, but the general consensus, Dr. Soll informed me, was that this temple had been based around the tomb of a priest known as Ptalantohtep.

My blood froze. That name. It follows me. It lodges in my thoughts. Dr. Soll continued to speak, but I heard none of it as Edgar's mad words came unbidden to my mind. The Earl had spoken both of Ptalantohtep, and cursed cargo. Of the dark evil that had lain within the *Endeavour*. How much had he known? Had he learnt of this mystery as I had, and sought out more? Had he too become inexorably engrossed in this riddle, until it consumed his mind and left him a maddened husk?

Seemingly unaware of my growing distress, Dr. Soll continued with his lecture. I was only half listening as he told me what local lore was known about Ptalantohtep. He had been a king or high priest, no source was definitive, in the earliest days of ancient Egypt. He gave the names of various periods, but not having made any study of history they meant nothing to me. Differing stories had him as either a great sorcerer or a cruel and vicious ruler. In either case, whatever his life had been, the actions he had filled it with were enough to ensure his name had lived down through the millennia. I was no longer asking questions, but Dr. Soll seemed happy to lecture me further with no encouragement. As I sat there he went on to the custom of sealing tombs with spells and curses. The primitive locals would still avoid archaeological digs for fear of such magic. He offered, if I was interested, to dig out and recount a few of those stories regarding this particular tomb. Finally able to find my voice, I hastily declined. I had no wish to know any more of this darkness than had already been awakened.

Desperate to be away from all the artefacts and curios from that damned continent, I thanked my guide and quickly fled the museum.

My mind is still reeling. The words of Earl Edgar seem once again fresh in my head. What had he done? What exactly had he known? What did he search for, and what did he find? What was happening?

Tomorrow I must pack my few belongings, but now I must sleep. The night is dark and I grow tired. My eyes are heavy, yet still I feel as if somebody's gaze is upon me. The darkness is oppressive.

Here! I had thought I would not find this journal again. I thought I might have thrown it out when I first moved to my new rooms back in October, as I have had no need of it since then. It was simply purchased to keep notes of my investigation of Earl Edgar, and further entries were more from habit than need. I have no memory of having unpacked it, and yet here it was sitting behind another book on my meagre bookshelf.

Now, with my situation falling around me and my mind wandering and confused, I found myself thinking of it once more. Perhaps, as has aided me before, the act of writing my thoughts on paper might allow me to filter through these confounded memories to make some sense of factors that otherwise go unseen. I am hoping that this, along with re-reading the notes I made at the time, might allow me to put to rest the fears and worries that have been stirred up by my visit to Buenos Aires. So much seems to consist of naught but coincidence and impossibility, that the guidance of some supernatural hand seems the only possible explanation. As sensible thought rejects this absurd notion I must seek out a logical frame for it. My brain fails to see past the unreality of it all.

Perhaps I should use some fresh book to do so, but it seems efficient to use this old thing. It already contains my notes of that time, and so will allow me to find any points that elude me. Carrying two notebooks around would be pointless.

Also, and more irrationally, I find I do not wish to spread these words and thoughts from these pages. I feel that I must keep them together, rather than allowing them greater freedom to further contaminate the world. I had truly hoped to forget those events I had chronicled within these pages. I believed I was beyond them. But I am wrong. They haunt me, and I can not wrestle my mind free of their insidious influence.

What has happened to me that I allow myself to indulge such childish notions?

I shall start, in order to arrange my thoughts, at the point where I made my last entry. With my advancement in the company, I was assigned new work regarding the business of the Leer family. It was a great boon for my career, and also meant I was kept busy enough that I spent little time thinking of Earl Edgar. However, some kind of mania had begun to grow within me. While most days I was as healthy as ever I was, on occasion some paper or invoice would come across my desk that would send my mind into a flash of recollection. Each time this happened it affected me more, until each attack would leave my concentration fractured for the remainder of the day. I would suddenly find myself unable to focus; my breath rapid and my pulse sour. All the mysteries and impossibilities I had encountered, and endeavoured to forget, would throw themselves back into the forefront of my mind and I would find myself racked with an unassailable panic.

When first this happened I was given some level of sympathy. Both my illness abroad and the stresses of my return journey were known by my colleagues and it was understood that for a short while small relapses might occur. But as these attacks continued to grow in strength the light in which I was regarded began to dim. If these attacks happened in the morning I could lose a whole day's usefulness. The sympathy I had been given by Mr. Dennings since my visit to Parrel House soon faded, and I could sense my slipping from favour. No matter how I fought to control my humours these attacks continued with ever increasing frequency.

I had never before displayed any of the symptoms of a nervous disposition, and yet so soon after my return from Romsey it was noted that I would jump and twitch at the slightest noise. I have developed a discomfort if I remain in crowded spaces for too long, and the feeling of being watched has risen to an uncomfortably pervasive level. I cannot sit still for more than a few moments without feeling those searching eyes on the back of my head. What is wrong with me? Why am I suffering so? Even now, as I sit at my writing desk, every few moments I am compelled to glance behind. There is no place within this room where any may hide, or to enter the door without my noticing. Common sense dictates there *cannot* be anyone in here with me, and yet I am unable to stop myself from looking.

My situation came to a head in early November. There was occasion for one of the other clerks to venture down to the archives, and the condition in which I had left them was discovered. When I had fled that room I had paused barely long enough to cram all the papers onto the shelves, let alone give any thought to their proper place. At no point had it occurred to me to return and rectify this. When the condition of the shelves and the disorder of the forms I had been reading was discovered, Mr. Caine and Mr. Dennings were furious. Quickly they went about deducing the culprit, and soon it became obvious I had been the last person to venture there. I was called into their study, and, in the state of panic I was in, I found myself wholly lacking the wherewithal to defend myself or concoct some ready excuse. I was told in no uncertain terms of my disgrace. Moreover, my constant attacks had led them to believe the extra responsibility had proved too much for my constitution. Whether it was some lingering effect of my illness or simply a weakness in character, the firm could not entrust such important dealings to one as unreliable as myself. Their decision was that I would be returned to my former position as a mere clerk.

What has becoming embroiled with the Leer family and their cursed histories done to me? I cannot forget those things I have read or heard, nor make any sense of the questions they throw up. I have read and re-read the words in this journal, desperate that some logical and clear detail might be revealed in its pages. Yet my hopes seem to have been for nothing. I go over the facts as I have written them over and over again, but can make no sense of the mania that has broken my career and left me in terror of invisible fears.

Monday, 2nd December 1816

It is another dark and threatening day. Despite my exhaustion I woke well before any hint of the dawn. Bathed only in the baleful darkness of the early hour I was struck with the absolute certainty that some other presence shared the room with me. I cannot explain it, as it was pitch black and I could make out no signs of movement. I am ashamed to say I panicked, and clamped my head under my blankets like some callow child woken from a nightmare. Eventually I chided myself for a fool and gathered the courage to face the agent of my paranoia. Throwing myself from my bed I scrambled to open my curtains. The faint light of the street lamps was enough to calm me and allowed me to check once again that I was indeed alone.

Today, as I left the office, I purchased fresh lamp oil and a number of good quality candles which I have placed around my room. As much as I hate this weakness that has grown within me, I cannot face the thought of waking once again in the dark as I did this morning. I fear my nerves are broken by this business.

My days are duller now than they have been, and I wonder if this goes some way to explaining my wandering mind. The demotion of my prospects with Caine and Dennings has struck me hard. If I had only had the forethought to return to the archives and tidy the mess I left, I might have saved myself. Yet I allowed these fears to control me. I have lost that advancement on which I had pinned so much of my future, and let my mind occupy itself with this debilitating mania.

Wednesday, 4th December 1816

Yesterday I was struck by another of my attacks and, giving in to melancholy, decided to drown my sorrows. Today I am regretting it.

Only an hour or so into my day, the door to the main room in the office was opened for just a moment and I heard Mr. Caine dictating a letter concerning the Leers. Only for the briefest moment could I hear him, but suddenly my mind was swamped with thoughts and memories and an irrational panic. It was too much for me. Air seemed to rush around my ears, while at the same time my breath became shallow and hard to catch. Wholly unable to hold myself in check I almost broke down completely. Those around me looked on with the derision I deserved. I felt a wreck. A pitiable mockery of a man.

I managed to somehow muddle through the day, likely to a far lower standard than I should have, and on leaving passed by the way of the local gin shops. While I have never practiced abstinence, neither have I been a heavy or frequent drinker. Last night I drank huddled and alone, the eyes of my fellow clientele resting on me. My misery was my only company.

Eventually I found my way back to my rooms. As I lay

there in my stupor, I found myself pondering on my situation with a new mind. Whether Edgar Leer had indeed been struck by some ancient curse or not, I cannot deny the fact that my involvement with his family has cursed me. My attacks had all taken place whilst dealing with the Leers. Perhaps if I could be free of them, I might be able to free myself of this mental affliction? I am young and resourceful and would soon manage to rise up once more from the lowly position I have found myself cast down to, whether with Caine and Dennings or with some other firm. I actually fell asleep in a far brighter mood than I had felt in weeks.

But my dreams? The dreams that assailed me last night remain with me now with a vivid, unreal recollection. It was a dream unlike the hovering nightmares I had previously suffered. I was in my cabin on the *April Mercy*, though not as it had been on the journey. The room did not toss and tip, but was sturdy as if stationed upon land. There was no door. All else was the same but there was no way for me to leave the room. How long I remained there in that prison of a cabin I cannot say, for time passed strangely as it often does in dreams. Nor did I seek out escape. In fact, I felt a strange peacefulness within me. I simply sat. Waiting. For what, I do not know.

I wish that sense of peace I felt remained with me now. I awoke this morning with none of the optimism I felt the night before. The subtle thoughts and creeping worries rest on my mind again. No longer do they come in sudden attacks, but grow like an infection. The words of Edgar's notes begin to float before my eyes with greater and greater frequency.

I go over and over these notes, desperately seeking some easy and mundane answer, but can find nothing. I know there is more to this than I can see! It cannot simply be in my mind. What is it? Something follows me. I am never alone, and I no longer fool myself into believing it is something of this world. I have come to the conclusion that if I trust my own mind then I must accept some outside influence as the cause for my condition. I am afraid. I believe I can only be free of this mania once I understand it more, and yet each time I have sought to make an understanding it has only led me further down the path of madness. Can there be an answer? Am I meant to know more? Am I capable? It has been almost a month since I have had any direct business regarding the Leers, yet my mind is assailed more than ever by this paranoia. Perhaps it is not they who hold this sway? Could it be they are peripheral? They must be included somehow. But how?

Tuesday, 10th December 1816

It is no good. I have tried to empty my mind of this whole affair but it is impossible. I had put this journal away, thinking it another symptom of my mania, but every moment I was in my rooms I could feel its presence, the urge to put my thoughts onto paper. Even in my childhood I was never able to simply give up on a challenge. Each task I have undertaken in my life I have surmounted. Since my last entry I have thought much on this matter, and have deduced that this trait of character is the cause of my distress.

The only conclusion I can see is this: my mind recognises there is some answer within this mystery, and without finding the solution it will not allow me to continue with my life. It is no weakness of the soul that afflicts me, but an inborn and stubborn tenacity. Until I can solve the riddle before me I will be unable to know peace. This is why these thoughts return to me each time I try to move on; my mind rebels at a task left undone.

I have read and reread this journal until I can almost recite it by rote. I have spent my evenings reliving memories, attempting to recall any facet of my travels I may have left out; some detail, perhaps, that I believed unimportant at the time. I know there must be something I have missed, some key that will unlock this puzzle.

In doing this I have come to certain conclusions that must be accepted, however strange and unseemly. Firstly; despite all rational belief, it must be accepted that there is something about this business that is not of this earth. There are things in this world we do not understand; occult and unholy things that we, in our quest for peace and sanctity, choose not to acknowledge. I must accept that the reason I have been unable to rationalise the things that have happened to me is because they are *not rational*. There is something else, something supernatural. Many would call me mad if my acceptance of this fact became public knowledge. There are some, I am sure, who already whisper that my mind was cracked by my travels, and who would take whatever excuse they could to have me sent to the asylum with the fools and the lunatics. Despite that, I must accept this simple truth. What answer is there other than madness?

And what about this presence that has followed me since Buenos Aires? Still I sense it. I feel it in the empty room with me. There is no rational justification for it. Since I know I am not mad, I must accept the supernatural element.

Accepting this fact brings such a clarity to events that have otherwise defied explanation. How else was the cargo of the *Endeavour* not lost as all evidence said it should have been? That the winds that followed me from South America culminated in that one great maelstrom in exactly the same spot as the other poor vessel sank? That which was put down to coincidence by my naïve insistence of the 'rational' must, upon examination, be recognised as some external and malevolent force. There can be no rational explanation but the irrational.

Seeing this, my mind has found a focus it has lacked for many weeks. I can see the goal that I must reach in order to regain my composure and my life. I must come to understand what it is that has happened to me. Only then will my mind allow itself to rest, and my life be my own again.

It is now clear that in my investigation into the last days of Earl Edgar I stumbled upon something far greater and more spiritual than I at first recognised. Something, some evil phantasm, has become attached to me. This is the architect of all my suffering and woes. To combat it, I must comprehend it.

My first step must be in holiness. My fall in circumstances has required me to find cheaper lodgings, and so I have found a room in a decent house on the edge of town, close by a local church. There I begin each day in prayer, that God might grant me protection from that which haunts me. In this action I find a peace that has eluded me for so long, but on leaving the building once more the attending spirit settles upon me. It grows stronger now, perhaps sensing that I have resolved to battle it. I can go nowhere without the certainty it is with me. I have purchased a small pocket bible. I had hoped consulting its pages might give me some protection whenever I felt most assailed, but it grants me little comfort. Still, I shall be strong. I shall not allow this thing to overcome me.

I am resolved now to what I must do. Clearly Edgar discovered the story of the cargo from the tomb of Ptalantohtep. He must have been struck by some curiosity, and determined to investigate. Before his settling in Buenos Aires he was known to travel on such whims. I know there must be records of his actions and movements at Caine and Dennings. I must search them out.

Wednesday, 11th December 1816

Nothing.

I hoped to begin my search today. The papers I need will be in the archives. Once I have done this I will be able to move on. But today both Mr. Caine and Mr. Dennings decided to work late, and with both in the office I was afforded no chance to do so. Obviously my privileges have been curtailed and I can no longer make a visit to the basement without being questioned as to my purpose.

The presence at my shoulder seems stronger today. I could barely sit still. Its observance of my actions is an almost physical sensation, as if someone had their face mere inches from my shoulder. Each time I turn there is no one there, but the moment I face forward again I feel it. Several times I was forced to resort to my bible to calm myself. I took a passage at random and read until the sensations retreated to a point where I could make the attempt to focus on my work.

I hear those around me whispering. I fear my behaviour has been noted. Try as I might to keep my countenance plain, I worry my intentions are known. They would not understand. All those within the firm know of my disgrace. They all know I have no business in the archives. I must do it in secret. The one benefit I gain from my disgrace is none find it too strange that I stay so late. It is expected that I should work the longer hours to regain my former place in our employers' favour. Yet I cannot be seen to be obvious. I must find proof before anyone can understand what I have come to understand. But with those two remaining, I could not stay too long without arousing suspicion.

I am strangely tired. I have only just arrived home and yet my eyes are heavy. So heavy.

Thursday, 11th December 1816

Last night I dreamed. Falling asleep almost as soon as I lay in my bed, I was quickly whisked away; my mind taken unbidden with images and sights that I cannot account for. It was dark, yet I could see well enough. All was stone, or was within stone. A great tunnel stretched before me, never ending and somehow both greater than I could possibly perceive and yet so small as to enclose me tight. I ran; both pursued by and the pursuer of some agent I could not define. Fleeting glimpses of half recognised faces swept past, always gone before I could turn to look. A sense of fear and urgency filled me. I felt mad. There was no control. The stone enclosed and surrounded me.

I awoke with the lanterns still burning, thank the Lord. The room was cold with the chill of winter yet I was drenched with fear sweat. I sat panting, staring into the lamplight as gradually the pounding in my heart subsided.

Once again, today I was unable to seek those files I require! Again my employers stayed late. All day they watched me, until I could no longer remain without building suspicion.

Friday, 13th December 1816

At last! Today I was able to begin my search. My employers are now away on some business. I again designed to work late, enduring the stares and whispers of my fellow clerks as they one by one made their way home. I know they suspect me of something. Why must they stare so? I keep to myself, as much as I can with this damned presence over my head. I am careful. I know this supernatural observer is with me night and day, but what if that knowledge causes me to miss some earthly spy. The thought has not occurred to me before. I must be careful. I cannot afford for any to discover my course of action before I can explain myself!

With our employers away, no others had any need or desire to work late and I was soon alone. Quickly I rose and locked the door so I would not be disturbed. I worked fast. I hoped to be done with my task in one session, for as much as it was necessary I still recalled the emotions that had burst forth at my last visit and caused me to flee those dark confines. Searching carefully through the files, I found very little that was of use. There was no detailed report on Edgar's life. What we did have were legal notices and invoices, those papers required for the management of the Leer estates. The most I had to follow Edgar's progress were forwarded invoices from countries around the world.

The last official documents bearing his signature were from 1806, the last time Edgar visited England. I could not discern exactly what brought him back on this rare visit, but it seems someone managed to get his attention long enough to present him with a selection of legal documents for his mark. Knowing what I do of the man, I cannot think he cared much for the contents or paid much attention and signed for little other reason than to be done with it. Most were regarding the sale of the family's holdings or other payment of debts. Much of what used to be the Leer riches had been sold to pay for Edgar's extravagant lifestyle.

My work was stilted, as the whole time I felt the presence in the room with me. My concentration suffered, for I feared both the spirit and some earthly agent that might be watching me. Should I be discovered I would likely lose my position within the firm entirely, and with it any chance to find what I required.

As it was, I was unable to locate any one piece of solid worth, but was able to make certain circumstantial assumptions that smack of the truth. I could ascertain that after leaving England for the final time, Edgar and his wife next travelled to Egypt in 1807. There were various invoices that look to indicate he planned to undertake something of an expedition. This must have been it! Whether he learned of it before or during his visit to England, this final expedition must have been inspired by the mystery of the *Endeavour*. I can find no other evidence that Edgar travelled anywhere else before appearing in Argentina, where I know he stayed until his death.

I felt an excitement at having these answers, but took my time ensuring everything was in its place before leaving. Despite my fears and growing paranoia, I had no wish for careless actions to catch me as they had before. I arranged each folder and ledger carefully until I could be sure no one could possibly tell I had been down there. It took some time, but eventually I was satisfied. I know they suspect me. I know they want me put away so I cannot solve this mystery. I will not let them catch me. Not this time.

Before leaving, one last impulse took me. This might be my last change to access these documents. What if I needed to refer to Edgar's notes one last time. What clues might remain that I might now understand? I could not afford to wait so long again. Finding the small bound volume I took it from the shelf. I fancy the risk of someone looking for it in the future is small. None other than myself has seemed to take any interest in it before now.

Emerging from the archives, I arranged my desk to give the appearance of my having worked late and then slipped from the office into the dark evening. A light snow had begun to fall, the first of the season. I hugged my coat about me. Eyes followed me as I walked. All along the way I felt the presence over my shoulder; a permanent and unwelcome companion that seemed to heighten the cold as I walked through the drifting snow. The chill seems starker and more full, and remains even though I am now indoors. Sitting close to the fire does nothing, which is simply another sign of my situation's preternaturality. What I lack is proof that can be shared with others.

I cannot say for sure, but I feel as if the presence is changing; becoming stronger, somehow greater than it was. It almost feels closer to me. More focused. It is no longer a peripheral sensation. It is more now; a haunting spirit that follows me as if latched to my soul. This is good, I think. If I can grow to understand what it is, I can battle it. I am aware. No longer do I allow myself to waste my efforts in denying that which is so obvious. I am awake now to my dangers.

I walk in a world set apart. I am alert to those things we ignore in our everyday, mundane lives. I look around me as I walk through the city streets and part of me wants to laugh. All these people with such narrow perceptions. So unaware of this larger existence. Just as I was. Happy to live with their own naive visions of life. I see so much more. I am witness to things they could not possibly comprehend even should I attempt to explain it to them.

I am full of envy for those happy fools and their comforting ignorance.

Saturday, 15th December 1816

My dreams continue harsh and unwelcoming. The indistinct horrors that began to plague me so long ago grow firmer and more real with each passing night. I lie awake, fearful of sleep. I cannot stand the darkness, even for a moment. Even finding myself in the streets alone is enough now to bring about a rising panic within my chest. Living in solitude, with neither family nor companions to accompany me, I am wholly unable to end my habit of lighting lanterns around my room. I tried last night to make a stand against the horrors that seek to assail me. I was unable to bring myself to extinguish even one. I stood trembling before it for a full half hour, willing my arm to extinguish the gas. Nothing. The fear holds my soul fast and I can do nothing but seek more answers.

Again I dreamt of that impossible corridor, its dimensions so unlike that of our own world. As I seem to both fall from and climb through its length, my senses reel. In the way of dreams, it is as if my nerves go beyond that which is human. Twice I seemed to be overtaken by something dark and… wrong. Each time I awoke coated in a sweat and charged with an overwhelming fear. Each time I would fall back to slumber only to be taken by the nightmares again.

Monday, 16th December 1816

Nothing was mentioned today about my expedition on Friday. I am sure my colleagues suspect me of something, yet still they do nothing. They watch me, leering with contempt each time I catch their eye. They mistrust me. Laugh at me. Judge me. I am certain they will turn on me if they discover my plans. Only of that can I be sure. I must be careful, lest they use this business to work against me.

Wednesday, 18th December 1816

Something is there. Something new to me. I can feel it balancing on the edge of perception. I know not what this is, but I am sure that it harbours no good intentions towards me. Someone knows of my venture into the archives last week. I am sure of it. They watch me, all of them. I can sense the thoughts behind those eyes. I have kept to myself these last few days, lest in some unguarded moment I give away some clue that shall lead them on to my plans. But still they watch. Still they wait. I begin to wonder if it is safe to continue working at Caine and Dennings. While this riddle remains unsolved I cannot allow any to oppose me. But then what if I need to learn more of Edgar, or any of his family? What then?

Despite the time of year, I am uncomfortably warm. Where others bundle themselves against the cold, I sweat and chafe at my garments. It is as if some humid cloud hovers around me, perceptible only to myself. Is it some kind of manifestation of this unwelcome spirit? Some strange power it has to affect the world? I do not know. But it is a reminder that I must not dally in my quest to uncover its secret. The chill winter air is the only thing that refreshes me, but I am unable to bring myself to leave my windows open in my own rooms, and in the office none of the others will hear of it. I must suffer through it. I have no other choice.

Thursday, 19th December 1816

I dreamt again last night of the impossible tunnel. Once more it haunted my night and lingered long into the day. But it changes. Each time I dream, some subtle alteration is noticeable. Where before I was always alone, now someone is with me. I could not see them, but I am sure as certainty they were there. I feel as if each time I enter the dream I am somehow more physically part of it. More *there*. Each night feels more real, as if my physicality within the dream grows stronger and through this I am able to perceive more. I am terrified. This is no natural thing. If I leave this matter too long before solving it, might I one night find myself more there than here? Trapped forever within the nightmare?

I am now certain someone within Caine and Dennings is working against me. I feel them staring at me as I work. I cannot catch them, but I know they watch me. I have kept to myself, speaking to no one for fear they might use my words against me. I keep a steady eye upon them all, trying to deduce which of them are conspiring so. Palin's eyes are on me always. Whenever I turn he is there. My guard has not been strong enough however, as it appears one of them has gotten behind my back. Today, Mr. Dennings, once my champion and mentor, took me aside and instructed me to return home. He told me he and Mr. Caine had become concerned with my appearance and general demeanour. He claims they fear I have been struck again by some winter illness. Someone has gotten to him. Was it Andrew Palin, dripping poison in his ear? I cannot be sure this late after the fact, but was it not Palin who discovered my action in the archives? Could that be it? After taking over my duties whilst I was in Argentina, did he decide on my downfall as his own path to advancement?

If I could have called Mr. Dennings on this facade I would have, but I must keep up my pretences for a while longer. Each day I am closer, I know it. I am not ill, but cannot share this burden with anyone.

Perhaps Dennings, and his partner Caine, being so long in the employ of the Leer family, know some fact about this business that I do not. This seems the most likely. Why else would they have sent me across the world on this wild chase? Why else could they be so easily turned against me? They know something! They must. The spirit hovers at my shoulder. Mocking me. How much it knows I cannot say, but I am convinced now it can perceive that which goes on around me.

I must move now to deduce what I may. Soon I fear it shall

be too late.

Saturday, 21ˢᵗ December 1816

It is nearly Christmas. The city moves and rumbles and goes on with the mundane existence it enjoys. Thousands of lives, all lived without any knowledge of the secret things happening in the world outside their own petty influences. Things they cannot see. Things they refuse to see. Fools. Oh how I wish I was one of them, still able to accept that which I had been taught was true.

I awoke yesterday morning once more sweating and tangled in my sheets, the horrors of the night refusing to fade from my mind. I must determine some way of obscuring these night-time visions, or else I fear for my sanity. My tortured nights have left me exhausted and I find it harder to think clearly with each passing day. This is becoming too much for me to take.

Seeking more knowledge, I made my way to the nearby church. As always upon entering I felt a lessening of the insidious presence on my soul. Yet this effect seems weaker than it has been before. The sanctified ground of the church is becoming less of a shield. Instead of praying, as has been my habit, I sought out the priest, one Reverend Patterson; a rotund man whom I had seen lead service but never spoken to directly. As I approached him he seemed startled, but was gracious and welcoming; treating me with a courtesy that has been lacking from those I have encountered recently.

I wished to discover from him more knowledge on spirits and hauntings, hoping as a man educated in theology he would know such things. I had to be vaguer than I would like. Were I too candid he would think me mad. Like the others who follow me. Without first understanding that which only I can understand, I worry none can help me. Instead I asked him simple questions, claiming an interest peaked by some overheard conversations. I added in a supposed worry for the soul of another, one whom I did not wish to mention by name for his own sake.

Reverend Patterson seemed genuinely sympathetic to the tale I spun. There was still scepticism in his eyes, but he did not dismiss me outright. I am not a great storyteller, and he appeared to sense the hidden truths I would not speak of, though clearly he believed enough of my tale not to have me thrown from the church. He insisted he was not a man of great knowledge on this subject, having never made a particular study of it, but would give me what advice he could. He spoke of how those things that men called spirits are actually known to be devils; forces of Satan sent to tempt and torture the souls of the innocent. He gave me vague words on how heathens worship in foreign lands. When I pressed him on ways to combat such things, he could only provide me with vague platitudes concerning prayer and trusting to God. I have done both of these things. Neither have helped me. I have already determined that only by rational thought and examination can I be freed from the irrational. I asked of the practice of exorcisms, hoping for some practical ritual I might undertake, but was merely given more vagaries that betrayed his lack of knowledge.

He now began to show signs of suspicion, and pressed me for more information on my situation. I should have known he would try to trick me. Even this priest thought to use my situation to his advantage.

As we sat there on the hard wooden pew, the spirit, which for a short while had been pushed to the back of my mind, once again grew in power. Having built its strength against the sanctity of the location, it fell upon my mind afresh. I felt chills spread through my body. My skin became clammy. My head swam, the priest's words fading into the background. I felt powerless. A hand on my shoulder. No one there. I could not think. It was as if something reached inside of me and clenched a spectral fist around my mind, deadening the nerves and sinews that granted me the very power of reason.

I vaguely remember staggering from the building. A panic had overtaken me. Never before had I felt its touch so strongly. It wanted me out of that church, and if I had not fled I do not know what may have happened. What did it mean? What does it mean? Did it sense my seeking a way to combat it, and so strike back at me? No. It cannot possibly have such focus. Can it? Could it truly possess such consciousness?

The sensations did not leave me on escaping the church. I recall only blurred images. I ran. I was being chased by something. Fearing what would happen should I be caught I kept to crowds, heading for the busier part of town. I fought desperately for control of my own mind. Passers-by stood away, thinking me a madman. If only they knew the truth. My truth.

I awoke in a gutter. Everything was a blur. I have no memory after my flight from the church. An empty gin pot lay by my hand and my head throbbed, so I must deduce that I drank myself into oblivion to seek escape.

I have now managed to spend some time thinking over the events of yesterday. I must not let panic overcome me. Clearly this presence that has haunted me since Buenos Aries has some level of consciousness. It knew that within the church I sought knowledge I might use against it. The power it has over me leads me to the unavoidable conclusion that religious or spiritual remedies are of no avail. I must set my colours to the pursuit of reason. I must understand more of this thing. I must.

One thing of note is I have no remembrance of dreaming

last night. The gin put me in a state of total unconsciousness. No dreams came to me. Could this be my emancipation? I have ventured out and procured myself a small amount of gin. I hope it is of a better quality than last night's offering, or at least how I judge it from the taste within my mouth this morning. Perhaps a smaller amount might relax my brain and defend it from my nightmares without reaching the state that would render me ill.

Sunday, 22nd December 1816

I was wrong. Last night the nightmare came again. I did not drink enough. I awoke with my head free from gin's ill effects, but reeling from the unnatural burdens placed upon me by this affliction.

Once more the dream has grown in detail and immersion. As I run through that stone passageway, the faces in the corners of my vision are now so much clearer, though gone when I turn to look. It was as if they run with me, or at times as if they were me. All of us running alone in that corridor, yet together. Most are unknown to me, but I am certain that once lady Maria's face sped past; thinner and looking more ill than when I met her, but yet almost certainly her. Another I believe was Edgar. I have never seen the image of his face in life, and there were no portraits of him at Parrel House, but I know it was him in my dream. There is a clear resemblance to Sebastian his son, but even without that familial look I would be sure of it. I cannot explain how or why.

I feel my time is running out; the clearer these dreams become, the more I lose myself. I look over and over these notes but can see no link to the answers I seek.

What do I know? Edgar knew something. I must find out what. And what he did discover in Egypt? All I can think of would be to enquire at the museum again. There was nothing in the files of Caine and Dennings, and I doubt the Leer family would be forthcoming with any of the information I need, even should they know.

Yes. I must return to the museum and speak to Dr. Soll once more. Perhaps he can direct me to the knowledge I seek. I will go there on the morrow. This cursed ghost hovers at my shoulder, waiting. I must gather my wits. He does not have me yet!

Monday, 23rd December 1816

Last night the dream was not so strong, but reduced to the vague horrors I suffered previously. Strange how I now find this reassuring. The amount I drank was more than I had hoped would be necessary, but I will do whatever I must to combat these visions. I have procured more gin. If I must drink to sleep soundly, then drink I shall!

My trip to the museum was less fruitful than I wished. The attempt was almost scuppered from the first, for as I arrived in the Egyptian chambers I discovered the mere sight of the artefacts was enough to send me into a rising panic. I nearly turned and ran, but managed to best my base fears and keep a hold of myself long enough to enter and seek out a curator.

People know something. They edge away from me as they pass. I have noticed this before but in the museum it was obvious. Visitors backed away as I approached, looking at me fearfully. Do they know something of my intent? What rumour has been spread about me? The man at Caine and Dennings. Palin. Has he set about tales of my supposed madness? Must I endure these as well as my supernatural oppressor? The earthly realm conspiring with the spiritual to hasten my downfall?

Finally locating someone to ask, I enquired after Dr. Soll only to be informed of his unavailability He has travelled to some university to give a lecture. My reaction to this news surprised even me, as an inexcusable rage rose up in my breast and I began shouting, slapping the wall hard with my fist in wild frustration. It took more than a moment before I could master myself. Fearing I would be asked to leave I begged forgiveness, citing a bad night's sleep and the disappointment of my thwarted plans. I was in luck, and the gentleman I spoke to was in a forgiving mood.

Enquiring as to whether there was anyone I might speak to about an Egyptian expedition in 1804 or 1805, I was led aside to the corridor outside the main gallery where the curator asked me to wait. I found a seat and remained there for a maddening amount of time. I could not sit still. My agitations drew repeated glances from passers by. I felt sure he was not going to return, or would do so with a policeman and doctor to demand my incarceration. I fought to block these thoughts from my mind, to ignore the stares of those who passed me with mocking eyes.

Almost without meaning to I found myself standing and wandering back into the room. I do not recall consciously making any such decision. It was as if some external force or call had struck me. I found myself once again surrounded by the captured and rescued artefacts of the ancient North Africans. This time I was not affected by the same feeling of panic as I had before, but instead a strange sense of familiarity. Where before they had been exotic and terrifying to me, suddenly they seemed as everyday as a kettle or ink pot.

I walked as if in a trance. I made no conscious decisions as to my movements, but moved when and where the urge took me. I do not know how long I wandered that room, but in the end found myself facing a stout wooden cabinet. Under a glass lid sat a number of curious clay fragments and tools fashioned from some metal or other. These all surrounded the main exhibit for this case; a broach. It was about the size of my open palm. The metal was ancient and tarnished, but must once have been of great quality to have survived in such a remarkable condition after all these years. Its shape was of a serpent curved around itself. It had originally had gems inset for its eyes, but only one of these now remained; one solitary red stone staring up at me, while the other socket sat empty and dull. I could not look away. I know it regarded me. Not just faced me, but regarded me. I sensed something I cannot describe. Or is it that I will not? Even I do not know. All I can say is some fascination brought me to lean in until my face almost touched the glass. I felt the presence of the spirit that haunts me grow; spreading around me, surrounding me, infusing me.

I cannot explain what I saw next. For all my ramblings in these pages about the spirit and the effects it has had on me, I still cannot face some of the truths I guess at. As I looked upon that twisted serpent I swear somehow it reacted to my presence. Through that one jewelled eye the spirit regarded me physically for the first time. I do not know how I know. But I know. My breath stopped. The jewel began to glow softly. I could neither breath nor move. The spirit regarded me and I felt it take hold. It had me.

I do not know how long it was before I finally managed to pull my eyes away. Free from its gaze, I felt my body fall under my own control once again. I drew in breath for what felt like the first time in minutes. I was panting as if I had been running, and only my grip on the case itself prevented my legs from collapsing underneath me.

Looking around, I sought out some glossary or description for the objects within. On a card in the front of the case, in neat handwriting, was a brief description noting that the contents were donated to the museum in 1807, having been unearthed in Egypt as part of the expedition to investigate a lost desert tomb, thought to be that of the High Priest Ptalantohtep.

That word! That cursed word that struck my eye and caught my soul. The text of that card remains burned upon my vision, floating before my eyes even now. The name that has haunted me with unseen and indescribable terrors ever since first I read it. From Edgar's scribbled words, it has followed me. Haunted me. Now it had found me, and I felt my strength fail.

A hand landed on my shoulder, and the spell that held me in place was broken. I spun around, screaming, and pushing myself away. My nerves had been dragged to breaking point. The man I had spoken to before had returned with another. He spoke, but I did not hear him. Only one word filled my mind. Ptalantohtep. I was insensible with fear. I could not even think. My vision twisted, the room spinning like a dervish. Pushing past them, unheeding of anything around me, I ran from the gallery. I stumbled through the streets, and it was not until I found my way home and soundly locked the doors with shaking fingers did my panic begin to ebb.

I have barricaded myself within my room. I cannot go back there. I cannot. I will deduce all I need from that which I know already. I can. I must. I do not need to leave here. I have candles and drink to last. He is waiting. I can feel his presence just beyond my walls, waiting for me. It still has not faded, not since I gazed upon that ancient charm. It was his. Was him. They must have found it in that cursed temple. Why did they do it? Why was that place discovered, and not left to rot for all time? Why was it brought forth to damn me to this inescapable, living hell?

Wednesday, 25th December 1816

Christmas. So many spend today worshiping, but what do they worship? A salvation that shall never come? Do they truly know anything? Did I? Do any of us? What goes on in that supernatural element of which we shall know nothing until it comes to claim us? We pray that our religion holds the answers. That by blindly following in faith we shall be saved from that which we do not know. I have not been saved. Religion is weak, and I am without succour.

I attempted church this morning. On this most supposedly holy of days I hoped I might find some peace. Is there even such a thing? Can we find holiness, or is it all a misguided delusion created because we know there is no true protection? Did our forefathers understand what I know now, and create religion to hide from it? These things are hidden from me, but what I do know is that when I approached the doors of the church I felt a cold hard grip fix around my heart. I could feel those fingers tighten around it. It is stronger now. Ever since it saw me in the museum its power over me has become more certain. It did not prevent me from entering; I sat at the back but could still feel the eyes of the congregation upon me. I could not sit still. The unwelcome gaze of those ignorant churchgoers lay over me. How much do these people know? I know they wait only for me to slip, for some ill timed word to give them the excuse to throw me to Bedlam. Or worse. I could not keep still. The grip tightened around my heart, mocking my fears and prayers as its chill spread throughout my body. I was trapped. Now I was there, I wanted to leave. The spirit would not allow it. It held me there. Mocking me. Letting me flounder in the last vestiges of what hope I held. I could feel it smile at me, just as the serpent smiled upon Eve.

I could not find the strength to leave until the end of the

service. It was as if the spirit was taunting me by forcing me to remain, separated from salvation by the encroaching boundary of its power. My discomfort was at such a degree that the moment the cold latch around my heart was released I ran. Pushing others aside, I burst out of the doors and into the cold, winter air. The smog was thick, and every surface slick with frost. I fell, and the impact on the hard ground seemed to dislodge the grip that held me. As I lay there I felt the inner cold, that moments before seemed to be on the verge of freezing my heart, begin to lessen.

I lay on the hard earth outside the church, gulping for air and waiting for the strength to stand. Just the briefest thought of returning caused a bilious lurch in my stomach. As soon as I was able to push myself up, I lumbered into a gasping run. Now at last I am barricaded within my rooms. Barricaded but not alone. The spirit is still with me. Mocking me. Waiting. I must not sleep. Sleep is when it takes me. My mind is cracking but I must not allow it to take me!

Friday, 27th *December 1816*

Drink is now my only saviour. For the last two nights my sleep has been dreamless. Only by drinking until unconsciousness takes me am I safe. I am little rested, but would accept a lifetime of exhaustion if it would grant me remission from these nightmares. I must keep up my supply. I will leave my rooms only to procure more gin. I cannot allow the dreams to take me before I have solved this mystery.

Edgar drank. So many people told me. How did I not see? He drank and imbibed all the day long until his mind finally went. Was he seeking the same relief as I? Did he too undergo these nightly terrors? The same curse? Did he also feel the icy grip upon his heart when he sought ways to free himself from this curse?

My one fear is that my means shall not be adequate to maintain my emancipation. Edgar could. He had his fortune to supply a lifetime of intoxicants. I have no such funds. I must determine a stronger, more effective solution. There are treatments used for the manic and the depressive, are there not? Perhaps the medicines utilised in the treatment of madmen might also aid me? Yes. As reason must be the solution to my puzzle, then chemicals must be the solution to my pains. If I could only sleep, I know I should be able to solve it all.

*Saturday, 28*th *December 1816*

I have procured for myself from a local chemist a modest solution of opium. Having never required the medicine before, I know little on the subject and was forced to speak with the proprietor in rather more detail than I wished. I described the basic nature of my symptoms; the insomnia and lack of concentration. He suggested a tonic proven, he claims, to calm the mind and sooth the nerves. I attempted to indicate the solution I wished to purchase was for another, but he seemed disbelieving. How much does he know? Too many people know things. He served me without much hassle or questioning, but how much can I trust the bottle? Could he have tampered with it? He would not even need to. I know nothing of medicine. Have I even been given that which I asked for? His assistant glared at me the whole time I was in the shop. A surly adolescent, the boy's eyes never left me. Even when he was out of my vision I could feel his gaze. What was he thinking? He's been speaking with the others who want me to fall. I know it. Now they know I have sought out this tonic they will know their undertaking to break my nerves is working. He is reporting to them even now. I am sure. Even as I left the chemist's shop and made my way home I know he must have run to tell them. I have so little time.

But should this tonic have the desired effect then I shall praise the chemist for the remainder of my days. I pray for a clean night and a way to escape my dreams. I have been unable to leave my rooms since I returned with the tonic, so sure I am they follow my every move. The presence lingers and I am followed by men also. If I can only escape I shall be free to move once again.

We float. Within the void that spreads throughout perception, on the edge of all that can be seen or heard or smelt or thought. A cave. Vast in its dimensions and insignificant. Smaller than a puff of thought and all encompassing. It is all, yet nothing. It fills our senses and I can barely discern it. If we concentrate it blurs and fades, yet if I relax it all becomes one.

There are others with me. We are all of us alone. Each of us surrounded by a greatest expanse of nothing. A thousand minds and a thousand hearts. One body. A thousand souls all caught in the preternatural snare. Trawling through time, snagging each by its inexorable pull. Some foolish. Some unlucky. All forever caught. Dragged forever inwards in every conceivable direction.

Some fought. I remember times I did not know. I can remember being those of us who managed to hold off the unrelenting force, little understanding the nature of what we battled. Some of us have neither understanding or conception of what I am. Some of us recognise the surroundings only too well. I know the cause and centre of this web, but also we do not. It is strange. I can recognise the knowledge of all that we endure is here within us but yet we have no nameable concept.

There is a strange perception. We at last feel the world as it is and always has been and always will be. This is the true expression. The true perception. The trueness of all. This is how we have always seen. Never had I recognised this before, being now brought here again for the first time. Have we been here before? Again? Time is strange. All is real and the ill defined and mistaken measurements of man are of no use here. Again. Before. No meaning. Lost. Forever and never. The same. All here the same.

I sink. At least we believe I do. All and none of us. Gradually we see it is not a cave. A tunnel. On and on it goes. Forever and nothing. We merely perceive. Narrow broken perceptions. Some of us did. Was it us? Now it is seen for what it is. Both and nothing. An entrance. An entrance we all recognise though I do not know from where or when. We fall within. Within waits that which drew us here. The power. Great power resonating through what we thought of as time but now see for what it truly is. Such small perceptions. Small. Such small minds as we had before. Alas for our foolish notions. It is as if simply being here grants me the knowledge to recognise that which we perceive. Our minds are still unwelcoming but have little say. Is it part of what we are? Have we moved in space? Do we merely see. So many questions to distil from these terrible answers.

The tunnel surrounds me and we fall along its length. So familiar. So familiar and yet unrecognisable. Parts of me do. We feel terror at the sight. I have no concept of that terror, but we do for some of us know and through them the knowledge is known by all. It exists within us. There is no self. We are here. We shall be here. We were always here. He waits. He has been waiting, even when he has been with me I know he has been here. Waiting for me. For us. Watching. Death is here, death that is not death. Life is not within our poor perceptions. Greater and nothing. It is the end and also never ending.

We fall. In the view of what we now understand as perception the eyes draw us in. Two not one. Both. All recognise the eyes. We know them. From a thousand times and a thousand places and a thousand thoughts we know them. The serpent. The tunnel grows narrow. Deeper. We cannot tear my gaze away from the eyes. Silent laughter. Why am we here? How did we find myself in this place? His grasp, his wide temporal net dragging ensnaring throughout what we once believed was time. Impossible to escape. His knowledge is our knowledge. Screams. Silence. Terror. Unknowing. Those eyes. Huge. Nothing. That mesmerise and draw me in. We scream. A hundred thousand screams all one. We fall. The serpent. The eyes. The tunnel. Falling. Rising. His reach...

Thursday, 2nd January 1817

My God! What am I? What is happening to me? I no longer know between that which is real and that which is fevered nightmare. Is anything true? I began this journal to track and document the facts of my employment. If nothing else in life I have been a rational and efficient man in all my doings. Yet can I even trust the words I put to paper? Was it even I? Who else could it have been? No, I do not wish to think it. This journal was to be my salvation, allowing me to sift through the facts as they were. To glean the kernel of truth from all the chaff of superstition and fear. To set my mind at ease. Is any of it true? Any of it? How can I even know?

I have no memory of the last few days. Not since Saturday last, when I fell unconscious from the seemingly miracle sedative given me by the chemist. From that point on I have no memory. Of neither dream nor waking can I recall one moment.

When I at last awoke, I assumed all was well and I had found the arbiter of my reason. I had no recollection of dreaming, and believed fully I had simply undergone a full night's sleep. Then, rising from my bed, I discovered my room had been thrown into a great disarray. The furniture was all askew and thrown about, as if some mighty brawl had taken place. My clothing was strewn and ripped. In the grate I found a large pile of cold ashes where my books have seemingly been set ablaze. Fragments of torn pages lay around, as if someone had ripped them madly from their bindings before burning. Soot stained the walls and floor. What pandemonium had taken place that night I could not say, for I had absolutely no memory of any of it.

I immediately sought out my landlord, worried that some intruder had gained access while I, sunk in opium induced slumber, had slept on. I knocked at his door, but on answering his eyes narrowed and I was angrily accosted before I could even speak. Confused beyond measure by now, I was berated for the apparent noise and violence that he claimed had been emanating from my rooms for the past four nights. Knowing that all had been in good order those last few days I interjected, stating my whereabouts and indeed interactions with him during the time indicated.

Angered further by my insistence that he was mistaken, he turned and grabbed a news-sheet that lay beside the door. He thrust it at me with furious excitations about the date. I glanced at it, and my eyes were drawn to the impossible words. My landlord continued to harangue me as I stared at the page. How could this be? Four days have passed since I slept.

Only half listening, I took in what I was being told. Since Saturday night, strange and violent noises had been issuing forth from my room. Screams and crashes that echoed around the building, drawing attention from my neighbours. On that first night, in the fear I was in some danger, my landlord and fellow tenants had attempted to gain access only to find it impossible. While the lock would turn freely, the portal itself refused to open. Against even the strongest force they could put against it the door stood firm. By daylight silence would reign, but at the setting of the sun each night the screams and cacophony would be renewed.

Shaken beyond anything I had yet experienced, I made attempts at pacifying the man. To no avail. He insisted upon my eviction. I have been given until the end of the day to take my leave from these premises.

My first thoughts were that the tonic had indeed been prepared incorrectly. Then it struck me that it must have been a purposeful dosage. The chemist's boy had run from the shop as I left. Surely he had followed me, learned of my address and returned to his masters. Knowing I would be sedated they would have no trouble entering my room. What evils had they perpetrated whilst I slept? Clearly, I thought, they had dosed me anew each day. Did they merely wish my eviction? No. They knew too much for such simple goals. They had plans, and I decided I must be away before any of these might affect me again.

It was when I had returned upstairs and began to go through the remains of my few belongings that I came upon this journal. Of the few books in my possession this journal is the only one that seems to have escaped the burning. All other papers or journals I kept have been torn and incinerated. I had assumed this book shared that fate, yet there it sat upon the shelf. Intrigued, I took it up and flicked through its pages. What if the intruders had made note of my movements and thoughts. If so I would have to move fast, for within this book is more than enough evidence to have me sent to Bedlam. A panic rose within me, but this shrank in comparison to the cold fear that settled on me when I came to the point that makes me doubt everything.

The last entry. I have no memory of it. Everything after my account of my visit to the chemist is something I swear I did not write. This strange and chilling account of nightmare visions, of this hallucination of hell, is not mine. Could I have written it in my sleep? I do not see how. The writing is choppy and scrawled, but undoubtedly mine. The ink is faded. In comparison to the rest of the entries it appears as if this last one was written some time ago. Possibly years. It is faded and pale, and the paper around it feels drier and more worn. This is impossible.

But the most terrifying thing is that the words seem too familiar. As I read them, and I admit it took me a few attempts, Edgar's fevered last words came to my mind. Is not the writing akin to that which I read upon those forsaken pages? What has happened to me over these lost days? Perhaps the tonic, upon stupefying my mind, awakened some subconscious part, as if like a sleepwalker. Maybe I did indeed dream. And wrote as I dreamt.

But then wherefore came this violence?

I immediately searched around for Edgar's pages. I had kept them with me, and none had come from Caine or Dennings to retrieve them. I hoped against hope they had perished in the fire as had all other paper in my rooms, but on investigation I found the folder lying neatly under my bed; bound as I had left it last, untouched by the disarray that marked the rest of the room. Pulling open the ribbon and throwing the cover aside, I shuffled desperately through the pages. The mad Earl's half formed and non-sensical ramblings stared back at me, taunting my shaken sanity. I felt as if it were my own mind staring back at me rather than that of a sick and dying old man. Somehow the words seem to make more sense to me now. Less illogical. Still the same, but somehow more familiar.

Then I found it, lost amongst the half blotted and ill-written letters. It had meant nothing to me before, but clearly something about it had caught my recollection. Now these words become so much more important.

Across two pages of the thick paper are scrawlings that seem total gibberish. Words and phrases follow each other around the sheets with no discernible pattern or meaning. I had not even studied these in detail before, though clearly it had stuck with me. Now I see the sheet has numerous repetitions of the word "serpent" and the phrase "eye of the snake".

Then at one point, in the middle of the pages, can be read the following line: "That tunnel. All. Us and Me. I am alone with all."

With shaking hands I dropped the sheets to the floor. What could this mean? Do I somehow share the same madness as Edgar? Was he haunted by the same ghost that follows me?

Thinking of the spirit that has been part of my life for so long, following and watching me, I suddenly made the terrifying realisation that it was no longer at my shoulder. For the first time in longer than I can remember, I felt alone. The feeling of being watched within my own room had left me. It was such a shock that I swayed violently where I sat.

It was gone! Was I free? Was I my own man for the first time in months? Was this destruction around me and my lack of memory a relic of some unknown exorcism? Some process or ritual driven from my mind by its own execution?

For a moment I felt hope rise within me but then, as I felt about my senses, I discovered a change in me. I could feel something new. Something different. The presence remains. It has not left me, but instead now hovers *within* me. It watches from my own eyes. As my fingers touch something it feels with me. It senses my words before I say or write them. I threw myself back into the corner. I feel as if I am laughing, but I am not. Is it him? This sense of duality should have felt alien to me, but part of my mind must have been taken by it for even as fear rose up fresh within me, I also felt an inexplicable sense of accomplishment!

What has he done? What have I done?

I quickly gathered what remaining things I owned that were still in one piece, and fled. Oh, how I wish I could have left my notes and Edgar's there on the floor, yet some mental urging pulled me back. I could not even think of stepping through the door without them. Their hold on me is tight. I cannot even say why I still write in this damned journal. Its purpose is long spent but I cannot rest without having written. I now see that the compulsion to continue with it was not my own, but his. Now I wish to stop, but I cannot resist the urge to continue. Poisoning the paper with these words. Is this how Edgar felt? Were his last hours spent in desperate battle with the need to fill those pages now in my possession?

I have found myself temporary lodging in the cheaper part of town. They are not grand, but they fit to my reduced circumstances and the door has a firm bolt. I must sleep, yet I fear to. Resorting once more to opium is out of the question, so I have once more procured a supply of gin. I sit with it now, the lantern burning, and I wait. I do not know how much more I can take.

Friday, 3rd January 1817

I am afraid. I fear now that my life heads inexorably to some predestined conclusion and I am convinced I shall never again find peace or freedom. I am afraid of my own mind. Or is it my own mind? Do I even have mastery of myself? Something, someone, claims as much a hold on it as I.

Since waking yesterday, I am certain the spirit has settled now within my soul. I can feel it. He watches through my eyes. Feels through my skin. He has been waiting. I see that now. I am no longer convinced my decisions are my own. Everything I do I feel as if… as if we both make the decision. Moment by moment he becomes more and I become less.

Drink no longer has any power to numb me. I drank to excess last night in the feeble hope of preventing more dreams. No avail. I cannot say whether it is the lingering effects of the opium tonic or that he is fully inside my mind, but last night the nightmares returned in full. More so. As well as those images and terrors that have haunted me these last nine months are now elements of other things. Things I cannot write of. I cannot even bring myself to think of them. Just letting my memory brush remembrance causes the bile to rise in my gullet. I can feel him laugh as my mind fights. Why can't I be free? I shall never be free!

I awoke well into the day, drenched with sweat. I could not move. I had no power over any aspect of my body. I was strangely calm, and for a while this felt the norm. As if I were used to having no control of the vessel that carries me. It was not for half an hour or so that an unease at the situation began to grow. Blood pounded in my eyes like echoing laughter. My breath heaved. Even recalling this sends me shivering. I am losing my body.

Eventually my panic rose to the point where nothing could prevent my fleeing. At last I felt movement in my arms and wrenched myself from the sheets, throwing myself to the corner where I lay huddled and sobbing.

How much am I as Edgar? So similar. The room. The fireplace. I stare at those pages and almost feel like they make sense to me now. So long ago, in that Buenos Aires room, I felt there was some meaning in these pages if I could just see it. I feel this again. I feel if I could tilt my head at just the right angle the writing would somehow come into focus. They are lain out around me now. This journal on my lap and those pages on the floor. So much madness, yet I can almost see the answer. I can feel the spirit looking from my eyes as if dangling the solution before me. It is not gibberish. I know it!

It is warm. So warm and dry in these rooms. January weather. It doesn't seem correct. I smell harsh, dusty air around me. A gust? Some gust of heated air ruffles the sheets before me. It is not natural. If I do not concentrate I find myself pondering strange things. Tombs and deserts. Rites and practices with no holy purpose. My surroundings will, for a moment, seem wrong, but when I focus on these thoughts they scatter away like dust on the wind.

The burning. The burning of the pages eats at me. Why did Edgar do such a thing? Wonder. Is the key lost in those that are burned? Why some and not all? All of my books were burned in my rooms. Except this journal and these papers. What burned them? Did I? Could I? Why? Carefully I took one of the old sheets and held it to the candle. I had expected some strong reluctance to come upon me from the spectre within. Nothing. No strange feeling of dread. No cold hand clenched around my heart. At once I screwed up my courage and thrust the paper into the flame.

It did not burn! I held it there for more than a minute and not even did the parchment singe. It did not burn! What magic, what dark sorcery has been placed here I do not know but the paper did not burn. In rapid succession I took each sheet and forced it into the very middle of the candle's flame. Nothing. No blackening or charring or mark of any kind! This is how the papers survived Edgar's attempted destruction to come to me. What is this? Why are these words spared by this devilish intervention while others were permitted to burn?

What of this journal? I curse the very thing and should have thrown it overboard as an offering to the sea that tried to claim me. Is it also so afflicted? Are my words on this matter forever stained upon this world by whatever magic imbues those faded pages? I cannot bring myself to discover. I could try. The candle is here before me. The flame hot. Yet I cannot. Is this some protective impulse from my possessing spirit, or am I simply too terrified of the truth? It survived the burning of my missing days. What would it mean if I could not? What does any of it mean?

I am lost. My mind is not my own. Things all around me. This is not as life is. I knew I would be free upon finding the answer. I never considered whether I would be capable of understanding the nature of that answer. I can almost hear the creature. It mocks me. It waits. I feel those jewelled eyes upon me. It knows. It knows what is happening to me. Waiting. Waiting for me to fall. Fall into that dark stone embrace. It knows and sees and feels and senses everything. It is me. I am it.

Edgar. It comes from him. Somehow. I do not know how and do not want to. Whatever this dark curse uncovered by the Leers, I wish none of it. I am it. They brought about the snake. The serpent's eye. The glowing jewel. Dark. Menacing. See us. All of us. I cannot escape it.

Saturday, 4th January 1817

I am lost. Gone. My mind is lost, and my body shall soon follow. I will no longer be the master of it. The spirit slowly consumes me. I feel him. He waits. Patient with the knowledge of years, he shall long outlast my fragile mortality. What can I do? I am as powerless now as I was months ago when his sights were first set upon me. Ignorance was no protection.

This body. There is a battle over it. I am losing. This morning I woke once again to the same paralysis. I was frozen, unable to wrench control of a single muscle. Yet a calm covered me. All seemed well. It felt not as if I were losing control, but slowly gaining it. My thoughts were not my own. As I lay there, my mind swam with images and thoughts that were wholly alien to me. Half formed hallucinations floated before my mind's eye. Of empty deserts and towering stone walls. Of crowds and of solitude. Of great power. I held great power within. Great. Terrible. I was… not me. I was something. Great. Greater than all I am. I knew more. Knew things. Impossible things. Things that cannot be known, but yet I knew them. The room smelt warm; the dry heat of high summer, with the dust of the baked earth filling my nostrils. I felt it on my exposed flesh. I was not in my rooms. Not in London. Yet where else could I have been? The thoughts and memories of the one within my soul bleed out and contaminate. Falling. So many others.

It was far longer this time before I could rouse myself out of those sheets; at least a good hour before I could run, fleeing my room bearing nothing but this journal and Edgar's words. I could not leave them. I wished to, but could not. I do not want this thing. I hate it. I curse its very existence. The words within it taunt me. Stark proof of my madness. Yet I am compelled to continue, cursing my own words as they scratch from the pen. I want to destroy it, to smear it to illegibility and wipe it from the world. I cannot. I have not the control. I cannot destroy it. Should I hide it, I am sure I would manage mere minutes before being compelled to retrieve it. What option does that leave me? I can see only one. Only one.

I have failed. Lost. Huddled here by the river I can see no other choice. I felt their eyes on me as I ran. They see me, I know they do. Are they right? No. They all seek my downfall. They cannot be allowed to do this to me. Edgar. Cursed Edgar why did you do this? What was my crime?! I cannot escape! I sought understanding and answers. I sought reason. There is none. Nature mocks me with the knowledge that knowledge is beyond our reach. The people I see all seem so happy. So unaware. It will come for them. All of them. The world does not understand what is coming, what has come, what has always been. Time is not as we perceive it. We are so petty and narrow. The all encompassing snare. Why? Why here and now and me? This fevered madness fills me. The air is cold and a light snow falls yet I sweat as if the sun burns above me. I cannot breathe. It is too much.

I must hide these words. I cannot stop writing, as if I must by some compulsion pour myself into these pages. Why do I still write? I cannot stop. Recording all I feel for some other to become ensnared? I flee from life yet this book remains. I can put it down for only moments. Cannot destroy it. Hide it. Yes hide it where none will find it. I have a place. I saw it in the streets but I must not think it. It shares my mind, feels what I feel. Blank. Must not. It will be safe. Must not return. Perhaps being separated will free me.

No. I am foolish. I will not be free. When I am done, the dark stone chamber waits. Edgar waits for me. All of them wait for me. What other option? We are all trapped. All destined for that close, stone, enveloping blankness I see in my terror. I knew those souls. That means I am already there. Already trapped. Already cursed. Why fight? Some try. Edgar tried. He lasted longer than I, but what did it get him? Months? Years? Decades? A lifetime? Hope is forgotten. Fate is all. Snared.

First the hiding. Then an end to it. That small victory is all I may find. My days are done. I accept that which I could not before. This has been my finish for so long, predestined by a force so much greater than that we see. So long decided. Denial is blindness. It is an end. An end.

I only pray I have the strength to leave the journal and not return. Strength? Speed. I must be done fast. Must not think. It comes. I go. At the end it goes. We all go.

Friday, 10th January 1817

My dearest Letitia,

Thank you so much for your last letter. Please reassure Mother I am well. London is not as terrifying as she continues on insisting to think. I have a good job, good friends, and good prospects. I am not living in some slum, nor frequenting any dens of iniquity. She has heard it all before, of course, but it seems she must be reassured, so reassure I must.

I am sorry I could not return home for Christmas, but the firm has been very busy these last couple of weeks, for reasons I shall go into below.

Today, all of us were excused work to attend the funeral of a fellow who used to work at the firm; one George Sandings. He's the one I told you about before. Seems he went a bit soft in the head and got into some trouble. An odd fellow, he always seemed a bit off since he returned from some errand in South America earlier this year. I worked with him for a short time, but never got to know him. He was a quiet man. Always twitching and looking about himself, and so intently focused it was unnerving. He had been let go from the firm a few weeks ago, after some business with him and the archives. They say he picked up some brain fever abroad that he never recovered from. I didn't really pay much attention. He was a nice enough fellow to work with. He kept to himself, but seemed solid enough. I suppose I worked with him more than most, but he did not socialise much. But his dismissal did leave the rest of us with a lot to carry on with.

But wouldn't you know it, last week his body was found in

the river. I'm not sure what happened, but according to those who discovered him he looked as if he'd been attacked by someone. Beaten bloody, by all accounts.

Anyway, after the service Mr. Dennings comes up to me and hands me a journal. Apparently it was found with Sandings' body at the side of the river, along with some papers he had stolen from the office. It was how the Runner identified the body. Mr. Dennings has asked me to look into the affair, and see what Sandings got himself into. Apparently he had been working on one of our bigger accounts, and they want to be sure he didn't do anything to embarrass the firm.

I've flicked through the journal. It just seems to be an account of his time in the Americas. I'll probably have a look through it and the papers he had with him over the weekend and make a start on Monday. There's no point in worrying now.

I'll write again soon. Give my love to everybody.

Your dutiful brother

Andrew

<u>Acknowledgements and Thanks</u>

I have a few people to thank for helping through the process of writing this book.

Firstly a massive thank you to my wife, Frankie. For someone who has so much to deal with herself, she is always supportive when I need to take myself away for a while and write. And also for the vast number of half finished drafts she gets to proofread before anyone else. Without her support this book would still be half finished.

Thanks to my little sister, Emily, for her amazing work on the cover. Throughout my childhood I often wondered if she would come in useful one day. And she has.

To my parents; who brought me up in a house of books, and didn't complain too much when I spent a large part of my childhood with my face buried in them.

I would also like to thank all my alpha readers. Getting their advice and spelling corrections was invaluable. Without them my ships would have been travelling all over the place and I literally wouldn't have had an ending:

Frankie Brand, Sue Brand, Robin Brand, Andrew Tucker, Joni-Rae Carrack

Thanks guys!

<u>**About the Author**</u>

Originally from Hampshire, Thomas H. Brand now lives and works in North London. He spends his time sitting staring at the computer screen or notebook page. He loves every moment. When he isn't doing that he can usually be found reading things other people have written instead.

Please visit www.thomashbrand.com for more of information.

If you enjoyed this book, or even if you didn't, please take a couple of moments to leave a review on your online platform of choice. I really appreciate hearing back from my readers. It really does help me out, even if you just leave a rating. Thanks.

www.ingramcontent.com/pod-product-compliance
Lightning Source LLC
Chambersburg PA
CBHW061218210726
48294CB00006B/1891